MORE THAN *Enough*

Lorna Seilstad

FEATHER HOUSE

PUBLISHING

Council Bluffs, Iowa

Welcome to
THE MOSAIC COLLECTION

We are sisters, a beautiful mosaic united by the love of God through the blood of Christ.

Each month The Mosaic Collection releases one faith-based novel exploring our theme, Family by His Design, and sharing stories that feature diverse, God-designed families. All are contemporary stories ranging from mystery and women's fiction to comedic and literary fiction. We hope you'll join our Mosaic family as we explore together what truly defines a family.

If you're like us, loneliness and suffering have touched your life in ways you never imagined; but Dear One, while you may feel alone in your suffering - whatever it is - you are never alone!

Subscribe to Grace & Glory, the official newsletter of The Mosaic Collection, to receive monthly encouragement from Mosaic authors, as well as timely updates about events, new releases, and giveaways.

Learn more about The Mosaic Collection at
www.mosaiccollectionbooks.com

Join our Reader Community, too!
www.facebook.com/groups/TheMosaicCollection

To Sandra,
my dear friend,
who has opened her heart and her home
to more than thirty foster children
in the last twenty-five years.

CHAPTER 1

Still ringing the little bell mounted on her handlebars, Fiona McGrath wheeled her sparkly scooter into the hospital room and drew to a stop. Her patient, an eight-year-old boy, didn't even look up.

"Good morning, Amazing Avery!" She watched the back of his shiny, bald head waiting for him to turn and acknowledge her presence, but he didn't move from his position in the bed. She didn't blame him for ignoring her, but it was her job as a child life specialist at Bryce Memorial to give Avery as normal a childhood as possibe.

Normal, that was, topped with a great big dollop of fun.

She adjusted her flower-bedecked pink felt hat and sighed audibly. "Oh well, I thought you might like to play with Buttons today, but if you're too tired—"

"No!" Avery rolled over, and his pale face lit with a broad smile. "Where is he?"

Fiona reached into the basket attached to the front of the scooter and lifted the floppy-eared therapy rabbit from within. While she retrieved a towel from the bathroom, she heard the familiar mechanical sound of Avery raising the head of his bed. When she returned, she draped the towel over the bed linens and then set Buttons onto Avery's lap.

Avery lifted the bunny and nuzzled him close. He stroked the black and white spotted fur coat. "Did you miss me, Buttons?"

"You know he was just saying that very thing this morning.

He said, 'Fi, I miss Avery.'"

Avery looked up at her and rolled his eyes. "Rabbits don't talk."

"Are you sure about that?" Fiona used her index finger to stroke between Buttons' ears. "Buttons here is a very special rabbit." She sat down in the chair beside the bed and waited for the rabbit to do his "magic" before speaking to her patient. "Rough morning, Avery?"

"I guess. I just don't want to be stuck in this stupid hospital, getting stupid blood. I want to be in school."

Her heart tugged. Most kids in Dunedin or anywhere in Florida would love to miss school, but this wasn't the case for the majority of young patients with long-term illnesses. They often felt life was passing them by. They missed their friends and the normalcy of school. Avery had been able to remain upbeat during his treatment, so she needed to thank the nurse who'd tipped her off to today's change.

She glanced at the IV pump where a bag of platelets hung, dripping through a line into Avery's arm. Chemo patients often needed blood transfusions and platelets when their counts dropped. It was a side effect of the chemo, and Avery was familiar with the drill. "Are you missing something important at school?"

"Free painting." He released a long sigh as he let Buttons' ear slide through his slightly swollen fingers. "In art. We were supposed to get to paint anything we wanted."

"Ah, I see." She placed a hand on Avery's arm. "I'm sure you're disappointed."

"Yeah, but I'm pretty used to missing things." His downcast toffee-colored brown eyes and the sadness in his voice said it all.

She swallowed against the lump in her throat. So many of her "kids" said something similar. Team sports, scouts, 4-H, carnivals, and school dances all had to be skipped. Everyday activities like physical education or math or art were missed just as much. She ached to give it all to them, but try as she might, her efforts to remind them they were kids, not patients, were limited. Her program here was still new, and there was only so much she could do.

Pushing the ache within her aside, she smiled. "Hey, I almost forgot to tell you my joke-of-the-day. What do you call a sleeping dinosaur?"

"What?" Avery smiled as if she'd already delivered the punchline.

"A dino-snore."

He erupted in a fit of giggles, and heat radiated through Fiona's chest. After another five minutes of bunny snuggles, her pager vibrated. She was needed in the emergency department. "Sorry, buddy, I have to go, but I promise to come by later." She slid off the bed and lifted Buttons from a tired, but happier little boy.

He leaned back on his pillow and brought his hands behind his head, skinny elbows protruding like giant ears. "Bring Buttons."

"Will do." She mounted her scooter and waved goodbye. Hopefully, the ER patient wouldn't need her help for an extended period of time. Avery wouldn't have to stay long for his transfusion and she had a plan.

Gabe Cavenaugh straightened his tie and flashed himself a toothy grin in the mirror. *You've got this.* His familiar pep talk did little to quell his nerves. Why had his boss, the chief financial officer at Bryce Memorial, asked to see him with such urgency? He walked down the hall and knocked on the door's metal trim. William Case motioned him inside, and Gabe took a seat in one of the chairs that faced his boss's desk.

Willing his pulse to settle, Gabe drew in a long breath and sat back. He studied the rotund man, hoping for a clue about what this meeting might entail. The fact that Mr. Case had summoned him wasn't unusual, but Gabe sensed something unusual in the air.

"Good afternoon, Gabe. You've been doing a good job, so I want you to handle this." Mr. Case pushed a folder across his desk toward Gabe. "And unless you're a miracle worker, you're going to have to make some difficult decisions."

"Me?" Gabe heard the slight catch in voice. "I don't understand."

"It's like this. The board has some cockamamie idea about value-based care, but they don't understand the hospital's bottom line. At the end of the day, the books have to balance."

"Yes, sir. And?"

"And they don't." Mr. Case leaned back in his executive leather office chair and heaved a sigh. "Or rather they won't unless you figure out a significant place to cut."

Mr. Case's emphasis on the word *you* was impossible to miss.

"Sir, while I appreciate your belief in me, may I ask why you're sending this situation my way?"

"We're in a particularly difficult position. Two years ago, some board members secured a grant to develop a child life program here. The first year, the grant paid for the Child Life Department's start up and the child life specialist's salary completely. The second year, it paid for half of the salary and most of the program's costs. This next year, we're expected to absorb the full salary and cost of Child Life." He leaned forward and clasped his hands in front of himself on the desktop. "Someone needs to convince the board this department should be cut."

"Again, sir, why me?"

"Because I'd rather not be hated. Doctors and nurses seem to love this feel-good, hand-holding program, but let's be honest, it's not really necessary for patients' medical care. If the choice is to cut two nurses or cut this department, well, it's pretty obvious who is more important."

Gabe opened the folder and glanced over the familiar spreadsheet. "Maybe there's another way—"

"I don't think so, but if you're so inclined, you have two weeks to find it." Mr. Case stood and waited for Gabe to stand as well. "You'll have to make the decision and convince the board to see things your way. I wouldn't give you this responsibility unless I thought you could handle it. You proved yourself when you dealt with the Dr. Epstein situation. Now, just be prepared to handle the backlash when you suggest the axe."

Gabe shook his boss's hand. "I appreciate your confidence in me. I won't let you down."

"Make sure you don't. I'm counting on it."

With the folder tucked beneath his arm, Gabe headed toward his own office. He sat down at his mahogany desk to study the folder's contents. A quick perusal revealed that Mr. Case had told him the truth. There was a shortfall in the projected expenditures in the approximate amount of the cost of the new Child Life Department, but what was Child Life? He'd never heard of it and had no idea what they did.

Still, if Mr. Case said it had to go, he really had little option. Case might make it sound like it was Gabe's choice, but he knew the chief financial officer was passing this off to Gabe so Case could maintain his good-guy image. If the board only knew the truth about the man they trusted...

He stopped himself. He shouldn't go there. All of his opinions were based on gut feelings. Instincts and feelings had no place in the world of finance. For the board to doubt William Case, they would need facts, and Gabe had discovered nothing underhanded. Case's number-one goal was Case, and as much as Gabe relished being the youngest assistant chief financial officer in the hospital's history, he prayed he would never end up like his boss.

He rubbed the ache forming in his neck. It would be easy for Case to axe the Child Life Program and never think about it again, but how could Gabe justify cutting a program he knew nothing about? What had William Case called it? Hand-holding and feel-good? Not exactly novel and life-saving.

Even if he did a little research on Child Life, Gabe feared the outcome would still be the same. He'd end up cutting this program because it had to be done. It was his job. It would be best for the hospital, and to be honest, best for him. Disagreeing with Case could cost him everything.

He drew in a deep breath. He couldn't do it. He couldn't make a rash decision without knowing what he was dealing with. Case had said it was his choice, and he was tired of not voicing his opinions. If this was in his hands, he needed to do things his way.

After securing the folder in his desk drawer, he headed out of his office. He stopped by his administrative assistant's desk and drummed impatient fingers on the desk's corner. "Where can I find Child Life?"

Gerri, an espresso-skinned woman in her fifties, looked at his hand. "And good afternoon to you too, Gabe."

"Sorry." He stilled his fingers. "Good afternoon, Gerri. Child Life?"

"Fiona's office is near pediatrics on the third floor. I don't think it's even marked, so you might have to ask." Gerri's warm voice held a note of amusement. "But good luck finding her. She works all over the hospital."

His brows drew together. "So, you've met her? What does she look like?"

Gerrie chuckled and waved her hand dismissively. "Oh, don't worry. You can't miss Fiona McGrath."

With the ER visit completed at last, Fiona hurried off the elevator and made a beeline for her office. She made a quick call to discover if Avery was still there. He was, but his transfusion would finish soon and then he'd be heading home. She had to hurry. In her professional opinion, Avery needed this as much as the life-giving platelets they'd given him today.

She made quick work of securing the objects necessary for her return visit. Because she had so much to carry, she wouldn't use the scooter, but she still needed to bring Buttons along. After all, he was to be the star of the show.

She tucked an easel and tablet under her left arm and lifted a basket of supplies. Maintaining her precarious grip, she opened Buttons' hutch and snaked her right hand inside. "Come on, Buttons. Don't play hard to get."

Thank goodness he came closer and she snagged him. He settled against her. He didn't seem to mind being carried in a rather awkward position under her right arm rather than in his basket.

Heart pounding, she backed up to her door, which she'd left ajar, and pushed it open with her backside. She glanced at the clock. Prep time less than five minutes. Good.

She whirled to her left and collided with a solid figure.

"Oomph." She fell backward, landing hard on the laminate wood flooring. Her supplies flew through the air—paper, brushes, and paints—and landed with a clatter around her.

"I'm so sorry, ma'am. Are you hurt?"

A man in a tailored suit offered his hand, but she caught another movement off to the side. "Buttons!" She pointed behind the man. "Hurry! Grab my rabbit."

CHAPTER 2

Buttons? Rabbits? Gabe wondered if he'd heard correctly, and when he turned in the direction this strange woman was pointing, he saw nothing. Maybe she'd escaped from the psych ward.

The woman scurried past him on her hands and knees and snagged a black and white bunny trying to make a getaway down the hall. She gave it a quick once-over. When she seemed satisfied that the rabbit was going to live, she pushed to her feet and jabbed the animal toward him. "Hold Buttons while I pick up the supplies."

He didn't want to upset her, so he took the bunny but kept it at arm's length. What was the protocol for escaped patients? Should he call the psych ward to come get her?

She snapped up a pink hat with a daisy poking out of the side and plopped it on her head. Then, she quickly flipped the askew legs of an easel back in place before filling the upturned basket with paints and brushes. Finally, she retrieved the large tablet of paper. "Come on. We can still get there if we hurry." She rushed off toward pediatrics.

Good grief. He'd have to follow her. He couldn't let a looney like this near the children.

The hat-wearing woman sped toward the pediatric unit, forcing Gabe to nearly run to keep up. Not an easy feat since he had to hold the bunny in front of him to keep from getting get fur on his suit. A wave of relief washed over him when he saw the monitored doors. Either the clerk at the desk would need to open the door or the person entering had to have an access card.

Then, to his astonishment, the door swung wide upon her approach.

The clerk at the desk looked up and grinned. "Hi, Fi. Looks like your arms are full. Need some help?"

"No, I've got it."

The clerk suddenly stood up as he neared. "Sir, you'll need to sign in."

Gabe stopped. Was she talking to him?

"He's with me." Fiona motioned with her head. "Come on and hold Buttons more securely. You know, like a baby. He's the most valuable member of the hospital staff."

Had he heard that right? The rabbit was on staff?

Maybe *he* was the one who needed to go to the psych ward.

The peculiar sweet antiseptic smell of the hospital's floors hit him, and he longed for his office with its sandalwood diffuser. He hated hospital smells and, for this very reason, he generally avoided the patient part of the hospital.

The crazy woman pushed open the door to a patient's room, and Gabe trailed in behind her. A smile blossomed on the face of the boy in the bed.

Hat Lady immediately began to set up her easel, the daisy bobbing with her movements. "Avery, I'm glad you're still here. I've got a surprise for you." She held up a paint brush.

"I get to free paint!" The boy slid to the edge of his bed.

"Yes, siree. Anything you want. Even Buttons." She motioned to the rabbit in Gabe's arms.

Avery scowled. "Who's the bald guy? Is he on chemo?"

The woman shrugged. "I don't actually know who he is."

She marched over and held out her hands. "My rabbit, if you please?"

Gabe deposited the rabbit in her outstretched arms, and immediately missed the warmth of the furry creature. "I'm Gabe Cavenaugh, the hospital's assistant chief financial officer, and you are?"

She stroked bunny's black and white dappled coat. "This, as you may have guessed, is Buttons." With a bright smile, she glanced at the boy who'd already smeared the canvas with two floppy ears. "And our future Rembrandt is the Amazing Avery."

Gabe brushed rabbit fur from his gray Armani suit. "But who are you?"

She doffed her hat. "Fiona McGrath, the hospital's one and only child life specialist, spreading happiness and fun to sick and injured children everywhere."

Gabe faked a cough in order to keep from laughing. They had a clown on staff. A full-fledged clown. She couldn't possibly be that valuable to the care team.

Cutting this program would be easier than he thought.

"No, you're not." Fiona glared at Mr. High-and-Mighty Good-Looking standing in front of her. If he thought he could do this without a protest, he had another thing coming. A girl didn't grow up in foster care without knowing how to fight for something she wanted. She crossed her arms over her chest. "You are not going to cut my department."

He shifted uncomfortably on the child-sized chair in her

office. "I don't believe that's your call. The board of directors will ultimately make that decision."

"Based on your recommendation, correct?"

He nodded.

Fiona placed both hands palms down on the small table between them. "Do you even know what I do?"

He glanced around the room. Fiona could imagine what he was thinking. Buttons' hutch, affectionately named the Flophouse, sat along one wall. Pictures painted by her patients lined another wall, and propped near the door was her scooter. Of course there were games and toys, but if he looked closely, he would also see the various types of medical equipment she used to educate her young patients before procedures. There was even a special doll she used to show them what they'd be facing.

"Apparently, you paint with the children, show them your bunny, and do whatever else they taught you in clown college." His baritone voice dripped with sarcasm. He pointed to her scooter. "And please tell me you don't ride that in the halls."

"What do you think?" Anger made the center of her chest burn. Tidewater-blue eyes or not, this man had a lot of nerve. "And I am not a clown. I'm a certified child life specialist. I have a master's degree and have completed a rigorous, examination-based program which included a six hundred-hour internship at John's Hopkins."

"So it's an extra special clown college. I apologize. However, I'm still afraid your painting program is not essential. I'll try to get them to keep the program through the fiscal year if you'll agree to just leave quietly."

Fiona clenched her jaw so hard she feared her teeth would

crack. This arrogant man had no clue what was and was not essential to the health care of an adult, let alone a child.

She closed her eyes for a second. *Calm down. Breathe. Focus.* "All right, I think we got off to a bad start, and I'm pretty sure this is your first encounter with Child Life, and maybe even with pediatrics, since I've never seen you before. Can we agree on that?"

"I've been up here a couple of times."

To pass out pink slips, probably. She brought her clasped hands to her lips and blew slowly into them. Her "kids" needed her. What could she use to barter with? *Please God, help me figure out what this man cares about.*

Quietly.

That was the word he'd used. He didn't want her to make a scene. Why? Because her program was the "baby" of two of the board members and favored by a lot of staff members.

She lowered her hands to her lap smiled sweetly. "Listen Gabe, if I make a big stink about what you're proposing, I'm pretty sure I can have this hospital in an uproar before you reach your office downstairs."

"Ms. McGrath—"

"Hear me out. I'd like to make a proposal." She paused to make sure she had the assistant chief financial officer's attention. "I want you to spend five full days with me and then, if you still think Child Life is not essential, I'll go quietly."

"I can't possibly spend five entire days with you. I have important work to do."

Her pager buzzed and she picked it up and read the display, but before she could relay the message, it buzzed again. "I have to go. Radiology needs me and so does emergency."

"Really? Both?"

"Yes, at the same time." She stood. "I know it's hard for you to understand, but I'm a very popular person."

"Five days?" His broad shoulders seemed to droop. Perhaps he was beginning to understand the influence she might have over the staff.

She lifted the scooter's kickstand. "Five days that will change your life."

"Or kill me."

She shrugged. "I guess that's a possibility."

"I suppose I'll see you sometime tomorrow then."

"Eight sharp." She wheeled her scooter toward the door. "And for heaven's sake, don't wear a suit."

Gabe glanced at the dress shirts hanging in his closet. The clown said not to wear a suit, but it wasn't like he had a red nose and oversized yellow shoes in his wardrobe. He thumbed through the selections and opted for a slate blue polo, emblazoned with the Bryce Memorial logo. Surely, that would make her happy.

Fifteen minutes later, he pulled his cherry-red Mazda out of his apartment's parking lot. The sun was bright, but the temperature was a perfect seventy-two degrees. Nothing beat Florida in January, especially northern Pinellas County. If he didn't have this meeting with the child life specialist this morning, he might be tempted to take a day off and go golfing.

He managed the steering wheel while peeling a banana, and the car filled with the fruit's ripe scent. He took a bite before flicking on the radio. The melody of one of his favorite songs came through the speakers, and he tried to sing along despite the banana filling his mouth. The garbled sound made him chuckle.

As he pulled into the hospital's parking garage, his mood soured. Usually, his morning drive was his favorite part of the day. He'd plan out his day and make mental "to do" lists, but today he found himself dreading the next few hours. He prayed that she wouldn't keep him for a full eight and a half hours. Maybe he could slip away after lunch or something. Surely, she'd understand he had other work to do.

He stuffed two granola bars from his glove compartment into in his pocket before pressing the lock button on the Mazda. He made a quick stop by his office to let Gerri know he'd be spending the day with the Fiona McGrath, but expected to be back in his office by noon. Gerri flashed a Cheshire Cat smile, as if she knew some great secret only the women of the universe understood. He glanced at his watch. Seven fifty-five. Even though he was tempted to ask a few questions, he didn't have time to query Gerri further.

When he pushed open the door to the Child Life office, Fiona was standing with a giant tube of bubbles in her hand. As if the bubbles were a baton and she was a disgruntled constable, she wacked the tube firmly against her open palm. "You're late."

He stared. Gone were striped tights, yellow shorts, and suspenders. And where was the hat? Instead, she wore a cream-colored blouse, ivy green scarf, and black slacks that hugged a rather attractive figure.

She grabbed hold of the bubbles. "What are you looking at?"

"You're—normal."

"Of course I am."

"But you look—uh—nice."

She rolled her eyes and moved past him. "If you're referring to yesterday, you should know I only dress like that on Wacky Wednesdays. Grab that purple bag and come on. We've got a lot to do."

He lifted the heavy bag and followed her to the elevator, still amazed by the transformation. Yesterday, he hadn't even noticed that the woman had shoulder-length hair, which was steaked like orange marmalade on a sunny morning. And had he seen a dimple in her cheek?

At the elevator, she poked the down-arrow button and turned toward him. "Our first stop will be Radiology."

"Whatever for?"

"I thought we'd check to see if you have a heart, Tin Man."

"I'm not shutting down your program because I don't have a heart, Miss McGrath."

"Fiona or Fi." She corrected. "And you're not shutting it down. At least not yet." She sighed like a parent did when they had to explain something to their son or daughter for the umpteenth time. The elevator dinged and the doors swished open. Inside, Fiona hit the second-floor button. "Let's start off better. Here's what I do. A child life specialist supports children and their families and helps them cope with the hospital experience."

"Okay." He could hear the skepticism in his voice as he dragged out the word.

They stepped out of the elevator and she continued the discussion. "I have three goals. I call them the three P's—preparation, play, and procedural support."

He waited for her to elaborate, but she said nothing. He shifted the purple bag to his other shoulder. "What's in this anyway? Rocks?"

"You'll see." She pushed open the door to Radiology and a technician in the hall waved at her. "Your patient is in the prep room. She's six years old and her doctor ordered an MRI, so it must be important." She passed Fi a paper.

Fi read over the sheet and, without a word, made a beeline for the room.

Gabe followed. "You were telling me about the three P's."

"No, I'm showing them to you." She stopped outside the patient's room. "This is the first one–preparation." She placed her fingers on the corners of her lips and pushed them upwards. "But before you go in there, smile. She needs a friendly face, not a living, breathing Mr. Clean."

Even though he should have been offended, he found himself grinning as he entered the child's room. Fiona introduced herself to the little girl and her mother. She explained that Gabe was spending time learning about Child Life. Fiona talked to Holly, the six-year-old impish blonde with brown eyes the size of acorns, about her t-shirt imprinted with the image of some Disney character in a glittery blue dress surrounded by snowflakes. When Holly asked him who his favorite princess was, he had to admit to a severe lack of knowledge in the Disney princess area.

Fiona giggled and launched into a song about letting it go. Holly joined in, and once again, he found himself wondering about Fiona's mental faculties.

"Do you know what, Holly? You get to be a brave princess because you're about to go on an adventure today. They're going to use a special machine to take pictures of you on the inside." Fiona took the purple bag and withdrew a wooden replica of an MRI scanner and a Barbie doll. She set both on a tray table. "This is just like the MRI machine they will be using to take your special pictures only it's little for Barbie. Yours will be big for you. See how it can slide back and forth?"

Fiona went on to explain that the camera wouldn't touch Holly and that it wouldn't hurt in any way. "You'll go to the MRI room and meet the technician who will take your pictures. See this." She drew her finger around the opening in the replica CT. "It looks like a donut, doesn't it?"

Holly nodded.

"Only the inside of this machine is like a tunnel. It's sort of like a rocket and you're the astronaut. And just like an astronaut, you'll have to get strapped in."

Holly's eyes grew wide. "Am I going to the moon?"

"No, we're just pretending." Fiona picked up the replica again. "Because the MRI takes pictures using a giant magnet, you can't have anything metal on you. The technician will take you down the hall and let you change into our special hospital pajamas. They will tell you to remove this pretty hair bow, but you can keep your teddy bear with you."

Fiona explained that the bed could be adjusted up and down and that it made clicking sounds when it moved. Next, she placed Barbie on the sliding table and wrapped the Velcro strip beneath it around the doll's torso. "Remember when I said you'd have to be strapped in like an astronaut? The bed in the MRI has a special soft seatbelt. It will help you be sure you're extra still during your pictures."

Holly's mother leaned forward. "Do I have to leave while she has her pictures?"

"No, you can stay close by." She gave the mother a reassuring smile, then turned back to Holly and the doll. "The technician will also put some cushions around your face and put another special seatbelt around your head to keep you extra still. They'll even wrap you in a soft blanket. When you're comfortable, they'll put earphones over your ears because the machine makes loud noises when it takes your pictures. The technician will talk to you in your headphones. He or she will tell you everything that is happening. You can listen to music or listen to a book, too, if you'd like."

Fiona told Holly that the technician would give her a squeeze ball to hold, and during her pictures would ask her to squeeze it if she was doing okay. "Because you're going to be still as a statue, you can't nod when she asks you if you're okay because you have to stay very still in the MRI. Just squeeze the ball. If you need to talk to the technician, you can squeeze the ball."

Gabe scratched his head. How did Fiona know all this about MRIs? Even though she explained it carefully, wasn't this too much information for a child to take in?

Fiona told Holly that every astronaut needed a helmet, and she'd get one too, only this one would have a special mirror so she could see her mom standing at the foot of the bed.

"After you get your helmet on, guess what's next?" Fiona leaned forward, her eyes full of excitement.

Holly shook her head.

"Then, the bed will slide slowly into the tunnel—and the machine will take your pictures. You'll hear some loud noises when it's taking your pictures. The machine chirps like a bird, pounds like a drum, and vibrates like a jackhammer on a construction site. Just remember, it's supposed to make those noises, just like a rocket blasting off makes noises."

"How long will it last?" Holly's mother asked.

"About as long as one or two of your favorite television shows, so make sure you get all your wiggles out before you get on the table."

Holly's mother stood up. "Can I hold her hand?"

"It will be easier to lay your hand on her leg to let her know you're there." She pointed to the replica. "Holly, are you ready to pretend you're the technician? Why don't you tell Barbie what's going to happen when they take her special pictures?"

To Gabe's surprise, Holly recalled what Fiona had explained almost word for word. Occasionally, Fiona had to prompt her on what came next, but the child's recall was amazing.

"Wow! You did great." Fiona stood and held out her hand. "Are you ready for your special pictures?"

Holly's head bobbed. Fiona opened the door and soon a technician came into the room and introduced herself.

"Thank you." The mother gave Fiona a hug.

"My pleasure." She squatted in front of Holly. "It was nice to meet you, Astronaut Holly."

Holly grinned, and then, without any tears, she took the technician's hand and marched away.

Gabe's thoughts churned. Fiona obviously had a knack with kids. Holly had hung on her every word. Still, it didn't mean her job was invaluable.

"So that's preparation?" He picked up the miniature MRI

machine and slid the table with Barbie strapped to it back and forth. "I admit she did seem better prepared for the test, but couldn't the technician do what you did or even a video?"

Fiona's brow scrunched. "Maybe, but there's more to it than you think. There's knowing the developmental stages of each child's age. A teenager, for example, might have a whole different set of questions than a five-year-old." She took the replica from him and laughed softly. "And a teen would feel silly strapping Barbie in. And there's assessing the parent's needs as well."

"But does it make a difference?"

"To Holly and her mother, it does." She turned serious. "Do you know what they did before we used to prepare kids? They sedated them. Any time a medical professional has to sedate someone, especially a child, there's an element of risk involved. This is safer for her and for the hospital."

Gabe scratched his head. Perhaps Fiona had a point. This serious side of what she did seemed to at least have some value, but what about all the other stuff? The Wacky Wednesdays? The scooter?

Her pager buzzed. She read the display, passed him the wooden MRI structure, and motioned to the purple bag. "And we're off."

He stuffed the model inside. "Where to?"

"To meet the magician."

CHAPTER 3

At the hospital cafeteria's salad bar, Fiona dropped cherry tomatoes on top of the hardboiled egg slices and spinach leaves she'd neatly arranged on her plate. She then added a sprinkle of cheddar and a spoonful of sunflower seeds, before dribbling a vinaigrette over the whole creation.

She glanced over at Gabe and saw that his tray was loaded with various selections, including not just one but two entrees, a bowl of soup, a bag of chips, and at least three desserts. What was he going to do with all that food?

Either the Bald-and-the-Beautiful was a big eater or a big baby. He'd whined when noon came and went, and they'd not taken time for lunch. She'd promptly informed him that if she was able to eat lunch at all, it was always later than that. An hour and half later, she'd finally taken pity on him after she caught him eyeing a pediatric patient's lunch tray as if it were a feast.

She paid for her salad, then made her way to a table near a window. Outside, planters proudly sported an array of brightly colored flowers. One of the best parts of living in Florida was that even during winter, there were kinds of blooms to enjoy.

She considered starting her meal without Gabe since it would probably take the cashier thirty minutes to add all the food on his tray, but remembered she was supposed to be getting him to support her program.

He set his heavy tray down on the table with a thud and pulled out a chair. "Sorry. You didn't have to wait for me."

"No problem. I imagine I'll finish before you anyway." She spread her napkin on her lap, but when she looked up, she found that Gabe's head was bowed over his food. She always said grace before eating, but was he doing the same? He was probably asking God to help him survive eating the pile mounded on his tray.

When she finished saying grace herself, she discovered him watching her. Their eyes locked until Fiona broke the connection. She wanted to ask him about his faith, but it was too personal, and they were more adversaries than friends. Best to stick to what was safe. She forced a lighthearted smile. "So, tell me about yourself, Gabe Cavenaugh."

"What do you want to know?" He plowed into his food like a starving man.

"Family? Friends? Tapeworms that make you eat copious amounts of food?"

He laughed, deep, warm, and full. "Okay, I get it. It's more than normal. I have a high metabolism. If I don't eat a lot, I lose weight, and then, believe it or not, my doctor gets onto me. Eating like this and trying to gain weight is really quite a problem."

"Said no one ever." She speared a tomato and popped into her mouth. "I hope you know you'll get no sympathy from me." She motioned to his desserts with her fork. "Some of us gain weight looking at those."

"Oh, that reminds me. This one is for you. I noticed you didn't pick any dessert up, so I grabbed an extra." He placed the plastic-wrapped brownie on her tray. "Life is too short to skip desserts. You do like chocolate, right?"

"I am a woman. It is my God-given inclination."

His eyes twinkled as he returned his attention to the food in front of him. Between bites, he shared that he'd graduated from the University of Florida just eight years ago. "My family lives Palm Harbor, about twenty minutes from here. Besides Mom and Dad, I have a brother and two sisters. And a dog, of course. His name is Cap'n Crunch. Your basic All-American family."

Her chest squeezed. He presented the facts as if folks everywhere had the exact same thing in their lives, but he had no idea that simply wasn't the case, especially for her. What would it have been like to have a normal family?

Before he had a chance to ask about her family, she needed to change the subject. "What did you think about Mack the Magnificent? I just love magic therapy. I think the kids respond to Mack incredibly well."

Gabe leaned back in his chair and popped the seal on the bag of chips. "You're right. The kids seemed to like him. He was entertaining and his card tricks were impressive. It was fun to see the kids respond when he included them in the act, like when he put one ball in that boy's hand and when the boy opened it, there were three. And I loved the ice trick, too."

"I hear a 'but' coming."

"Forget it, Fiona. I don't want to upset you." He stuffed several chips in his mouth and bit down with a deafening crunch.

"I'm not that prickly. Just tell me what you honestly thought."

He took a swig of Coke. "Okay. I think it's really nice that you want to entertain the kids, but I don't see it as critical to their medical care. How much did it cost to have him come, anyway?"

Fiona clenched her teeth. She would not spout off. She would stay calm. Of course this pencil pusher didn't understand, but she had to open his eyes.

She drew in a long breath. "It didn't cost anything. Mack is a volunteer. And for your information, magic therapy is being used at over two thousand hospitals and rehab facilities

He leaned forward. "How so?"

"It focuses on engaging the patient, works on the child's motor skills, helps with their self-esteem and social interaction, and most of all, lets them be a normal kid instead of patient for a while. Have you ever been in the hospital as a patient?"

"Who? Me?" He took a bite of his brownie. "I had to get stitches once in second grade, but since my mom was nurse, she pretty much handled all the sports sprains and strains."

She had to get his attention, so she placed a hand on his arm. "Then it's important that you try and put yourself in the shoes of these kids. It's hard. Some of them have spent more time in the hospital than out of it. If we're going to treat the whole person, they need to be children first and patients second."

He dropped his gaze, seeming to ponder her words. Was she making progress? Was his icy heart beginning to thaw?

Then, before he could respond, his phone beeped. He whipped it out and appeared to check the messages. "Fi, it's my office. Do you mind if I cut out early today? I've got some important stuff to do."

Every muscle in her body tensed. She wanted to explode and shout that this was important, but she couldn't afford to alienate him. Had she made any progress at all today?

Hot tears pricked her eyes, so she waved a dismissive hand at him. "Go. I'll see you tomorrow."

He stuffed the last bite of his brownie into his mouth and gathered up his tray. As he walked away, fear pooled in her stomach like a lump of bread dough. What if she failed to win him over to her side and he shut down the program?

Gabe stepped out of his Mazda with an extra bounce. Yes, these new Nike trainers would be perfect while cycling. He moved to the back of his car to unhook his Schwinn.

"Breaking in some new gear?" His older brother, Chip, glanced down at the sneakers, then continued to remove his own bike from the rack on the back of his SUV. "Guess I'll have to take it easy on you."

"I'll be fine." Gabe set his bike down and checked the tires and brakes. He withdrew his helmet from the backseat of his car and secured the chin straps.

"If you say so." Chip made the similar checks, put on his helmet and mounted his bike. "Ready? Twenty or thirty miles?"

"Thirty. I had to sneak out early to get here, so let's make it worth it." The two began a slow warm-up ride, then fell into a steady pace on the Fred Marquis Pinellas Trail. They liked to start outside of Dunedin and take the trail to Tarpon Springs. By the time they returned, they'd make a full thirty miles. If they felt like a longer workout, they'd start in Clearwater or St. Petersburg.

Hunched over the handlebar, Gabe found his rhythm. Since he and Chip rode two to three times a week together, they had a similar cadence. Although neither of them were currently training for a tour, both had competed in the past. Perhaps they needed to consider entering a competition. He could use something new on which to focus—besides Fiona.

He looked around the area and soaked in the tree-lined trail. The former railroad corridor was now a safe place for cyclists, walkers, skaters and joggers.

They passed the historic Andrews Memorial Chapel, a little hundred and fifty-year-old church surrounded by a matching white picket fence. It even had a little arch over the entrance. He'd seen more than one happy couple leaving the church as he rode by after pledging their lives to one another. He wouldn't consider himself a romantic, but it would be a great place for a wedding.

When they passed The Boxcar Café, Chip pointed out that the once closed restaurant appeared to be open again, and maybe they could stop on the way back.

Riding through the city, Gabe found himself observing the residents on the sidewalks and streets. Winter's cooler temperatures seemed to bring everyone out including the old and the young. A child in a wheelchair playing ball with his dad made him think about the children he'd met at the hospital.

He kicked up his pace and attacked the bridge, making a steady whump, whump, whump sound as he drove over the bridge's wooden slats. The kids had really gotten to him today. Watching their smiles with the magician was, well, magical. It wasn't fair of her to make him tag along with her. Of course, sick kids tugged at his heartstrings. He wasn't made of stone.

"Tough day?" Chip pulled up alongside him.

"Yeah."

"Just take it easy. Your rhythm's off. We've got a long way to go."

Gabe slowed and forced his pedaling to match his brother's.

"You want to talk about it?"

Gabe gave a sarcastic chuckle. What was he supposed to tell his Mr. Law Enforcement brother? *I got unnerved by a crazy lady, some sick kids, and a clown?* His detective brother would haul him off to the looney bin.

"Who is she?" Chip asked.

"What makes you think it's a she?"

Chip shrugged. "I know you."

Gabe focused on his breathing. Steady. In and out. In and out. *Forget about the kids. Forget about the day. Forget about Fiona. A nice, smooth speed.*

"So, you going to tell me what's got you in such a state?"

Chip was not going to let this drop. Maybe it was his detective's sixth sense, but he always seemed to know when Gabe was keeping something hidden.

"There's no great mystery. I've been asked by Case to tell the board we need to cut a rather popular program." He skirted a pothole in the trail. "It's been a grant-funded program and this year, we were supposed to be able to support it. Case says we can't, and he says the program isn't necessary."

"What one is it? And how is it unnecessary?"

"It's called the Child Life Department and the child life specialist is a rather unusual, rather vocal young woman named Fiona McGrath. When I went to tell her I'd be suggesting Child Life be terminated, she threatened to get the staff in an uproar unless I spent the week finding out what she does."

"Sounds fair. What does she do?"

Gabe chuckled wryly. "As far as I can see, she spends a lot

of time playing. The first day I met her, she was dressed like a clown, and today, she brought in a magician."

"So her job is to keep the kids happy?" Chip shifted gears as they began to climb an overpass.

"She says there are three P's to her job: preparation, play, and procedural support."

"But you're not impressed."

"I spent the day with her. She's funny and honest, and she really connects with the kids. She does help prepare them for procedures, but I just can't see how this program is medically necessary. Can't the nurses do what she does?"

Chip shrugged. "I don't know, but you know who you should ask."

"Mom."

"She could give you an outside medical perspective. Why don't you mention it at supper tonight?"

Gabe squirted water into his mouth from a water bottle. "Maybe I should. But what if she's on Fiona's side?"

Chip laughed. "I guess that's a chance you'll have to take."

CHAPTER 4

"You want me to do what?" Fiona stared at Gabe until the hospital elevator dinged and they stepped out on the third floor.

"My mom just wants to talk to you about your program, and she doesn't take 'no' very well. If you don't come, she'll hound me until you do."

"Gabe, I don't know. I'd feel strange." Fiona waved her badge in front of the control, and the door to pediatrics swung open. Her stomach had knotted at the mention of eating dinner with his family. How could a girl like her relate to the perfect All-American family?

"It's just a relaxed barbeque in the backyard, and it will consist mostly of letting my mom talk your ear off. I told her about your program, and with her being a nurse, now she's curious." He pushed the door open to their first patient's room. "And I'm the one who should be worried. She'll probably be on your side."

Fiona hadn't considered that possibility. She could use an advocate. Maybe one night of discomfort would be worth it if she could convince Gabe's mother about the importance of the Child Life Department, but what if it backfired?

She turned her attention to the teenager in the bed. The girl wore a long dark braid that rested on her pillow. "Good morning, Liz. How are you doing today?"

It didn't take long for Fiona to assess Liz's state of mind. Even though Liz's window sill was filled with bouquets of flowers and balloons, she seemed upset since the doctor had told her that she wouldn't be out of the hospital before the weekend. "My birthday is Saturday. It's my Sweet Sixteen. It isn't fair."

"You're right. It's not." Fiona sat down next to the bed while Gabe perched on the corner of the couch. "What were you going to do?"

"I had my party all planned. It was going to be elegant. Not little kiddish. Everything was going to be in gold and blush pink." Liz fisted the blanket on the bed. "All my friends were coming, and I got a gorgeous dress to wear."

Fiona smiled. "Can you reschedule it?"

"Probably. But it's not the same."

"No, it wouldn't be." Fiona knew better than to try gloss over Liz's disappointment. "I'll talk to your mom. She can at least bring up a cake."

Liz didn't look up. "That would be nice."

Fiona stood and patted Liz's arm. "Don't give up hope."

When they exited the room, Gabe said nothing. He also remained quiet throughout the rest of morning rounds. He didn't ask any questions, so Fiona didn't explain how she assessed the state of mind and individual needs of each of the children in her care. She would have told him that after rounds were finished, she'd decide what she could do support each of them and their families during the child's hospital stay.

"Do you see every kid?" he finally asked.

"I sure try to. It's a case by case basis. Some need education and some need distraction. And most of them need to play." She led him back to her office. Inside, she began to fill her purple bag with a variety of toys and teaching materials. "And right now we're headed back to Wesley's room."

"The five-year-old hooked up to all those machines?"

She nodded. "Did you notice his three-year-old little brother? He looked scared to death. I need to explain to him why there's so many machines in the room and how they are making him better."

"How can a three-year-old possibly understand what's going on?"

She swung her bag over her shoulder. "Oh, ye of little faith."

He stared at her, dark brows scrunched with an unspoken question. Apparently, the blue-eyed genius hadn't thought she knew any scripture. She brushed past him and headed back to peds. Gabe would have to see this encounter to believe it.

His phone rang and she heard him stop to answer it. He motioned for her to go on without him. "I've got to take this. I'll catch up with you."

Disappointment washed over her like the evening tide. How would he ever come to understand the contribution Child Life made to the lives of the families if he bugged out all the time? She sighed and passed through the door to peds. With or without Baldy as an audience, she had a job to do.

Gabe tracked down Fiona in Wesley's room just as she was finishing up. "Sorry. That took longer than I expected."

"Wesley, Timmy, Mrs. Anderson, this is Gabe Cavenaugh. He's been shadowing me." She motioned to a chair. "Come on in. Timmy can give you a tour."

Gabe hiked a skeptical eyebrow, but sat down to listen.

Fiona grasped Timmy's tiny hand. "Can you tell Mr. Gabe about Wesley's medical equipment? Why is this one here?"

Timmy started off shy, but with Fiona's encouragement, he rattled off that the IV pump gave Wesley medicine and he even pointed to the tube to indicate how. He told Gabe the tube in his brother's nose gave him air and made it easier for him to breathe. "And this one," Timmy pointed to the heart monitor, "tells the nurses how many times Wesley's heart beated."

Gabe glanced at Fiona and smiled. "Good job."

"Tank you." Timmy crawled up into his mother's lap.

"Mrs. Anderson, call me if you need anything, and Timmy, keep up the great work." He gave the child a fist bump.

In the hall, Gabe leaned against the rail on the wall. "How did you do that?"

"I let his natural curiosity take over, and then, I let him do a little medical play with my doll." She wiggled the fabric doll in her hand and the arms and legs flopped around. "I find it's a great combo for the little ones."

"But he wasn't even your patient."

"The whole family is my patient. My job is to help them all cope with the hospital experience."

Gabe fought the pride welling in his chest for the work Fiona was doing. Even if he didn't think it was entirely necessary, he had to be impressed with how well she did it. They started to walk down the hallway. "So, what's next on the agenda?"

"Do you remember the three P's I told you?" She stuffed the doll in her bag.

"Is this a quiz?"

She chuckled. "Sort of."

"If I get it right, can we go get lunch?"

She rolled her eyes. "That sure of yourself?"

"I am." He stroked the whiskers on his short-bearded chin, then lifted his hand to count off the recitation. "The first was preparation. That's when you prepare the child for what's going to happen. The next was play, and you seem to be really good at that. And the last was—uh—procedural support. You haven't shown me that one, yet, have you?"

"No, I haven't. And congratulations. You got all three." She glanced at the clock on the wall. "Lunch first and procedural support second. Let's drop my Mary Poppins bag off on the way to the cafeteria. I recommend, however, that you try to leave a little food for the rest of the staff today."

"Funny lady."

She grinned and raised her eyebrows. "I try."

When they reached the cafeteria, Gabe suggested they eat their lunch at one of the outdoor tables. After he'd paid the cashier, he located Fi seated in the sun with a sandwich and an apple on her tray. The sunlight made her soft marmalade waves glisten. He tried not to stare, but he didn't think he'd ever seen hair the color of hers. Freckles, he'd noticed earlier, dotted her nose, and he hoped that given her fair skin, she wouldn't burn sitting out in the sun.

"Earth to Gabe." She waved to him and drew his attention.

He hurried over, sat down his tray, and pulled out a chair. "Sorry."

"Is something on your mind or is your blood sugar that low?" She pointed to his heaped tray with her fork. "Eat up. I can feel the weight melting off you as we speak."

He offered a quick prayer and dug into the broccoli and beef he'd selected. The ginger aroma wafted to him on the outdoor breeze. After he'd downed half the entrée, he came up for air. "Hey, this food reminded me. Have you thought any more about eating with my family tomorrow night? They live in Clearwater, so it's not far."

A spark of fear appeared to flash in Fi's eyes. Why? He was the one who should be afraid. And was it possible for Fiona's already light face to pale even more? Dinner with his family was really no big deal. Maybe he should let her out of this, but his mom was really looking forward to speaking with her, and she'd keep pushing him until she got to meet her.

Fi tried to bite into her hero sandwich but couldn't quite get her mouth around the width of it. Lettuce, tomatoes, and mustard squished out and splashed onto her navy t-shirt. "This is just great." She grabbed a napkin and swiped at the mess. "Look what you made me do."

"Me? How?"

"You got me thinking about all this family stuff—and then this happened." She made another vain attempt at removing the mustard, then finally crumpled the napkin and tossed it on her tray. "Sorry. That wasn't fair."

"Forget about the picnic. The idea obviously distresses you." He knew he sounded petty, but it irked him. After all, it was just a picnic. It wasn't like he was asking her on a date.

His heart thudded. Wait a minute. Maybe she had taken it the wrong way. Maybe she thought he was asking her out. But surely she knew he couldn't even if he wanted to, which he did not. Did she think he was pressuring her?

Oh boy. He was in trouble. How was he going to get himself out of this one?

To his relief, the ER paged Fiona right after she'd taken the last bite of her apple. He, on the other hand, had a whole entrée yet to devour. She motioned to the take-out containers station. "You'd better grab one of those. We have to go. A toddler needs stitches."

He considered telling her he needed to eat, but he could tell by the look on her face, she was in no mood to listen to excuses. Less than fifteen minutes later, they arrived at the ER with Fiona's purple bag in tow.

Phil, one of the ER nurses, smiled broadly when he spotted Fiona. "I'm so glad you're here. This will be a hard one if you can't keep him distracted." He eyed her purple duffle. "Got your Mary Poppins bag, I see. Good. You're going to need it."

They followed Phil into a treatment bay and he introduced her as the hospital's child life specialist, or better known as the lady with the cool toys. She talked calmly to the mother, and learned the toddler was aptly named Chase. Apparently, Chase had "chased" their puppy through the living room, but had lost his balance and fell into the corner of a coffee table. The doctor had told Chase's mom that the laceration on the top of his head would need stitches.

Phil signaled her that he was ready to start, so Fi pulled out her first distraction toy, a light spinner. "Watch this." She moved the spinner around out of Chase's reach while Phil removed the dressing on Chase's head and prepared the area for suturing. The blood-drenched dressing made Gabe's stomach roil.

"Hey, buddy, you better sit down." Phil motioned his head

toward a stool.

Fiona looked over at a pale-faced Gabe and shook her head in disbelief. "Chase, what colors do you see?"

He rattled off red, blue, and pink and she let him have a turn holding the spinner.

When the doctor joined them, Fiona pulled out an *I Spy* book to keep Chase's interest while they numbed and shaved the area. He didn't seem to notice at all. She then withdrew a dinosaur puppet and sang songs with it to distract the boy while they cleaned and sutured the wound. What else did she have in that bag?

"All done." The doctor stood up and pulled off his gloves. "Chase, you did great." He gave a nod to Fiona. "And once again, Miss McGrath, we're in your debt. Someday, you're going to have to let me take you to dinner to say thanks for all you do."

Was this doctor hitting on Fiona? He stood and frowned at the man, irritation growing with the man's flashy bravado. Sure, Fiona was amazing, but this was hardly appropriate.

She returned the puppet to her bag and zipped it shut. "Dinner isn't necessary, Carlos. It's my job and I love it."

Gabe said nothing until they were waiting for the elevator. "I can't believe the nerve of that doctor. You know you could turn him in for harassment—asking you out in the work—" He stopped, his mouth suddenly dry. Did she think he'd done the same thing?

"Relax. Dr. Carlos Abrantes is a nice guy and he's harmless." The elevator doors swished opened. "And at least he doesn't get queasy when he sees blood and, more importantly, he appreciates what I do."

The words hit like she intended them to. She'd been amazing in there and yet, he'd said nothing. So far the day hadn't gone his way. Score? Fiona-3. Gabe-0. He always liked to win, but at least he still had a few hours to get things swinging in his favor.

"So," he asked, "what's next?"

"Blush pink party favors, pink decorations and as much pink as we can cram into a hospital room." Her eyes lit as she considered the possibilities.

"Liz? Sweet Sixteen and never been kissed?" Unconsciously, his gaze dropped to Fiona's mouth, where she was biting her bottom lip between her teeth. He swallowed hard and then met her gaze.

She grinned with a glint in her meadow green eyes. "About the never been kissed part? Her, yes. Me, no."

CHAPTER 5

Fiona slipped a "Sweet 16" label around a miniature candy bar and secured it with tape. Chuckling to herself, she looked across her office to where Gabe was working. "How are the vases coming?"

Gabe held a brand-new urinal aloft with an open-ended handle and a flip top lid. "What made you think this could be a vase?"

She shrugged. "I use what we have."

So far, what they had was bag full of candy bars now bedecked as favors, a large sign on which she'd painted "Happy Sweet 16!" in pink letters, and a dozen daisies waiting for the would-be vases. Gabe, she had to admit, had been a good sport about the whole affair. But he'd found using an X-Acto knife to slice off the tops of the four plastic urinal bottles to be a bit of a challenge.

"There. I'm done." He sat down at one of the child-sized chairs. "Now what?"

She brought over a couple of yards of fluffy pink tulle she'd saved from a baby shower she'd given for a friend. "If we had more time, we could douse those urinals with glitter, but I guess we'll have to settle for adding tulle bows. Are you up for it?"

"Just kill me now." He swept his arm around the room. "All of this pink is sucking the masculinity right out of my veins. I'm too tired to move, and I have an unexplainable craving for chocolate."

She rolled her eyes and joined him on a matching tiny chair. "All you need is a piece of tulle about this long." She cut a swath and slipped it in place. "Then, you wrap it around the neck of the...

uh...vase, tie it in a bow, and *voilà*, it's ready for the flowers." She cut the stems of the daisies and added three flowers to each urinal vase. "See? It can hang on the side of her bed rail. She'll love them."

"If you say so." He made a feeble attempt at tying a bow. "You sure her mom is coming with a cake?"

Fiona nodded and perfected his creation. "And bringing some of her girlfriends."

After the next bow, she pronounced him a hopeless bow maker and finished the task herself. He was relegated to adding the daisies. A knock on the office door came just as she finished the last bow.

Liz's mother peeped in. "We're here. Is the party still on?"

"Absolutely." Fiona hurried to the door and swung it open. Besides Liz's mother, she found six young ladies, arms full of gifts and balloons, waiting in the hall. She flashed a smile at them. "Are you all Liz's friends? Thank you for coming. It's going to make her day." She told Gabe to gather up the vases, while she put the favors in a basket. Then, she asked two of the girlfriends to carry the banner in.

The pink parade made its way to Liz's room, but Fiona held up her hand outside Liz's door. "Let me go in first and make sure she's ready for guests. If I give you a thumbs-up through the glass, then you all come in. Okay?"

A few minutes later, she gave the signal and the crew filed in singing "Happy Birthday." Liz's face split with a broad smile. Her eyes brightened as she watched her friends hang the banner on the wall. Her mother set the pink dotted cake, complete with layers of pink frosting ruffles and tiny gold dragees, on Liz's tray table. Hoots of laughter erupted as Gabe slid the "vases" over the safety railings.

"This is all so sweet of you. It's perfect." Lizzy beamed at each of them. "Thank you."

"Present time!" One ponytailed friend placed a gift bag on Liz's lap.

As Liz opened her second gift, Fiona glanced at her watch. She took hold of Gabe's arm. "Time to go."

"Now? But what about cake?"

"Lord forbid I deny you sustenance. You don't have to leave, but I have an appointment." She turned to her patient. "Sorry, Liz I have to cut out early. Happy Sweet Sixteen."

"I'd better go, too, then. We stick together." Gabe turned to leave.

"No, stay." Fiona pressed her hand on his chest. "Really, it's fine. My appointment isn't at this hospital."

Gabe's first-floor office felt like a haven. The dark wood, the black leather, and the familiar items on his desk seemed to welcome him home. He inhaled the sandalwood scent from his wax melt, sat down in his ergonomic chair, leaned back, and closed his eyes.

He was exhausted.

Going over the day, he considered all that had happened. Watching Fiona work with kids was something to behold. Time and time again, she pegged what they needed and delivered it even in the most stressful situations. Even though he still wasn't sure someone else couldn't do what she did for the most part, he already knew no one could do it as well as she did. Sure, she was unorthodox, but he didn't mind it so much now.

His feelings about her had changed, but was she manipulating him? They'd only spent two days together. Maybe she'd set him up by handling cases that she hoped would tug at his heartstrings. It was hard not to be moved by cute kids and grateful parents.

He wished he could get someone else's opinion. If Fiona had agreed to come to the family picnic, it would have been great in that respect. His mom would have spotted any falsehood in a split second. No one could pull one over on her. Besides, her experience in the medical field would have been an asset.

Then again, the invitation had created its own problems. Had Fiona misconstrued his invitation to the picnic? If they weren't in this awkward situation with him preparing to recommend cutting her program, he might look at her differently. No, who was he kidding. He and Fiona McGrath were not a match in any way, shape, or form. She was more likely to fall for a hippy than a financial officer.

But she had made that comment about kissing.

He sat up straight and opened his computer to check the messages Gerri had left for him. Enough Fiona thinking. He had work to do. Work, that because of Fiona and her crazy plan, was not getting done.

Scrolling through the messages, he noticed one from a board member who'd helped with the original grant to fund the Child Life Department. Had she somehow heard about what was being considered? Fi had promised that if he spent five days with her, she wouldn't make a fuss. But in all honesty, he couldn't blame her if she'd called in the big dogs.

Good grief. Why was he thinking about her again? He

organized the notes by urgency and picked up his phone to return the first call, an appointment he'd have to cancel.

He sucked in quick breath. Appointment. Fiona said she had an appointment but not at this hospital. Did she have one somewhere else? Was she already looking for a new job?

A bur of irritation dug deep. He tried to return to his tasks, but two thoughts surfaced over and over like a bobber on a fishing line. First, she should have had the decency to wait to look for a job, and second, he shouldn't care, but he did.

An arrangement of fresh flowers sat on the table in the waiting room of her therapist's office. Fiona bent over to smell the roses and drank in the sweet scent. She loved roses.

"Hello, Fiona."

She turned at the sound of her therapist's voice. Laura Batista had on a pair of fun, red rimmed glasses. Fiona thought the petite woman in her late fifties owned a different pair for every outfit. She often imagined her saying, *The better to see you with, my dear."*

"New glasses, Laura?" Fiona took a seat on her favorite comfy chair. Besides the new spectacles, Laura sported curly gray hair. In the last year, she'd come to realize that Laura's unassuming presence was a façade. She might look like a granny or a librarian, but she was more like a bulldog with a bone.

Laura walked across the room and opened a door. "I thought we'd go straight to the sand tray today."

Fiona couldn't believe it. If her session was going to include sand therapy, there was usually some precursor activity. And although she often spent time in sand tray therapy with Laura, Fiona figured her therapist could probably tell by the look on Fiona's face that they needed a serious conversation and not relaxing time with sand. Fiona knew better than to question Laura. The woman always had a reason for what she did.

In the sand tray room, small book shelves full of miniatures lined the walls. There was a little bit of everything including tiny dollhouse people, superheroes, fantasy figures, monsters, dragons, bridges, castles, and sea shells. There were animals of all kinds, nets, and even a tiny cage. Since Fiona knew the routine, she sat down at the table and began to let the white sand trail through her fingers, imagining the stresses of the day washing away. She loved the feeling of the sand, and it didn't take long for it to work its magic. She now felt calmer, more centered, and more grounded.

As a Christian therapist, Laura didn't adhere to new age hype, but she did believe that nature was one way God healed souls. Feeling this sand between her fingers, Fiona had to agree.

After a minute or so, Fiona smoothed the sand in the table to a flat plain, then began to add contours. She looked up when she'd completed the mound in the middle of the tray.

"Would you like to make a scene in the sand today?" Laura asked, holding out a small basket. "Remember, don't think about what you're selecting. If something reaches out to you and speaks to you today, put it in the basket."

Fiona nodded and went to the shelves. She scanned the top shelf and was drawn to a building. She added it and a plastic lightning bolt to her basket. Then, she found herself picking up a lighthouse and a set of knights on horses, jousts at the ready. She dropped each item into her basket. Finally, she picked up a turtle, a dragon and a clown. All seemed intriguing.

She returned to her seat, and began to set up her scene. Laura had instructed her many times not to overthink it. She'd told her to simply let her mind go, and play. In fact, Laura had said it was Fiona's childlike ability to play which had already helped her heal considerably from her childhood.

Fiona placed the building with the lightning bolt jutting from a crack on the top on one side of the mound. She examined the blue knight in her hands. He had a white cross on his chest. She jabbed him into the sand on the other side of the mound, and then picked up the red knight. She laughed to herself when she removed the knight from his horse and replaced it with the clown. She added the joust. This odd couple would face off.

She still had three items left—the lighthouse, the dragon, and the turtle. She put the lighthouse on top of the mound and set the turtle inside the building. But where should the dragon go? She looked at the scene and set it on top of the building.

There.

"Now, let's take a few minutes to just be present with your creation." Laura sat with her hands on her notepad.

Fiona stared at the scene. She knew what would come next. Laura would ask her to tell her about her scene, and Fiona would most likely spill some dark secret from her childhood that she had no idea was tied to what she'd just made. There were plenty of secrets to spill.

"So, do you want to add anything else to your scene?"

Hmm. Laura didn't ask that every time. Fiona nodded and stood. She padded over to the shelves. She wasn't drawn to more animals or the shells, but the feather meant something to her. She selected it and a handful of yellow stones. When she returned to the tray, she added the feather to the center of the mound and then surrounded the lighthouse with the yellow stones.

Silently, she wished her counselor good luck. This was going to be a whopper to analyze. But she knew Laura wouldn't give her answers. The reason sand tray therapy worked was because it was the client who assigned meaning to the symbols, not the therapist.

Laura leaned forward and pointed to the unnamed structure in the box. "Fiona, what's this building?"

Fiona eyed the building again. "It's the hospital."

"And why is there a turtle in it?"

"It's a 'Shell Station'?" she quipped with a grin.

Laura appeared to bite back a chuckle. "Fiona, humor shows you're a divergent thinker and it helps you cope, but in here—"

Fiona sighed. "I know. I know. I can't use it as a shield to keep from delving into important things." She looked at the turtle again. "He has a shell. I suppose he's safe."

"And the dragon?"

"He's fierce. He's the great protector."

"Of the turtle?"

"I'm not sure yet." It was an honest answer and Laura didn't press it further. Fiona reached out and touched the lightning. Her eyes widened. "This week at the hospital, I suddenly found out my program might be cut. It was like a lightning strike. The turtle might represent my kids or my program."

"Or possibly yourself?"

"I don't think so. I think on that side, I'd be the dragon. I'm fighting for them." Fiona pointed to the clown on the horse. "On this side, that's me."

Laura peered over her glasses and scowled. "Really, Fiona, a clown?"

Fiona covered her mouth with her hands to hide her laughter. "I wasn't trying to be funny. Honest. It fits, but you're not going to believe this."

Laura gave her a professionally cordial smile. "Try me."

"I made a deal with the man who wants to cut my program. He doesn't think it's important. He called me a clown because it was Wacky Wednesday, and you know how I dress up for the kids that day. The clown comment must have been in my subconscious."

"So, you're a clown fighting a knight?"

Fiona cocked her head to the side. "But I'd hardly call him a knight. I should have made him a monster."

"But you didn't." Laura sat quietly for a few seconds. "Why do you think that is?"

"Poor character selection?" Fiona tried to keep things light, but Laura didn't fall for it. Fiona sighed. "I guess I think he could change his mind and save the program. Deep down, maybe that's what I'm hoping for. Maybe it's a fight to the death."

Laura pointed to the lighthouse and the feather. "Tell me about those."

"The feather is easy. One of my favorite Bible verses in Psalm 91:4. 'He will cover you with His feathers and under His wings you will find refuge.' I could sure use some refuge right now and I've always liked the image of God covering me with soft, downy feathers. It feels so safe. My mother was like that when I was little, but later, well—you know."

"And this?" Laura pointed to the ceramic lighthouse

surrounded by yellow stones.

"Lighthouses give direction to the sailors telling them where to, uh, go, right?" Fiona rubbed the back of her neck.

Laura tapped her pen on the notepad. "You could have said that they show the safe harbor or where to land, but you used the word 'go.' Are you questioning where you should go?"

Good grief. How had this come out? Fiona blew out a breath through pursed lips. "It's more like whether I should go. The knight guy asked me to a picnic with his family so I could talk to his mother about what I do. She's used to be a nurse, and she's curious. On one hand, if I go, perhaps she would become an advocate for me and my program, but on the other hand, it's his family, and you know me and family. I'm not exactly the girl-next-door. I could never fit in and it's weird."

"And as we've talked about, you were in the foster care system. Sometimes children who grew up in that situation tend to push people away. I want you to keep the possibility that you're doing that in mind." She pointed to the lighthouse. "I see you picked yellow stones to surround the lighthouse. Why? Do you think you're a coward if you don't go?"

"No! Yellow is the color for childhood cancer. For me, it's the bravest color." Fiona picked up a rock in her hand. "Don't you see? This whole scene says that I have to fight for my kids."

Laura smiled. "Apparently, you gave yourself the answer you needed about going to the picnic. Next week, I want to hear how it went."

CHAPTER 6

Following the directions given on her cell phone, Fiona made a right-hand turn onto Saint Croix Drive in Clearwater and scanned the houses. Palm trees lined the street filled with ranch style homes with two car garages. It was the perfect neighborhood for the perfect family. She almost made a U-turn. Why was she doing this to herself?

For the kids.

She stopped in front of the address she'd found on the internet for the only Cavenaugh in Clearwater and said a prayer that it was the right home. According to the online site, the homeowners, Joseph and Victoria, appeared to be the right ages to possibly be Gabe's parents.

After she parked her electric blue Kia at the curb, she checked her apricot lipstick in the rearview mirror. She climbed out carrying a bowl of watermelon, feta, and mint salad, one of her favorites, and walked to the door, her shoulders scrunched with stress. If it wasn't the right place, maybe she'd just give them the salad anyway and go home. Better yet, maybe she'd leave the salad on the doorstep and do what the teenagers called a "ding dong ditch."

As tempting as that was, she rang the doorbell. Inside she heard movement and a male voice yelling, "I'll get it, Mom. I'm already in here."

What if it wasn't Gabe? What would she say?

Before she formulated a thought, the door opened and

she took in the figure in front of her. A gray t-shirt bearing an American flag stretched over a well-formed chest.

"Fiona!"

She lifted her gaze and released her breath. It was Gabe. In the flesh, or rather in cargo shorts and flip flops.

"I'm sorry. I should have called or something, but I changed my mind at the last minute and remembered you said your parents lived in Clearwater, so—"

He held up his hand. "I get it. I'm glad you came." He motioned her inside. "My mom will be thrilled."

The entryway opened into a white and gray living room that could have stepped off the pages of a magazine. A patterned area rug in muted colors sat atop a driftwood-colored laminate floor. A soft yellow designer chair offered a pop of color, and throw pillows added warmth to the space.

A border collie stuck his nose in Fiona's hand, and she bent and gave the dog a generous rub down. "Captain Crunch, I presume."

"The one and only. Crunch, let her be." The dog hung his head and walked away. "Mom's in the kitchen, and I want to introduce you to her first." Gabe's voice was warm. He seemed genuinely glad she was there, and Fiona began to relax. Maybe this would turn out okay.

The kitchen was a blend of white and gray with brushed nickel fixtures. Two oak bar stools sat at the island and the scent of baked beans filled the spacious area. A woman in her fifties stood at the counter adding spices to uncooked hamburger patties. She didn't turn around. "Gabe, who was at the door?"

He pressed his hands to his mother's shoulders. "Turn

around and see."

She cocked her head to the side and smiled. "And who is this?"

"Mom, this is Fiona McGrath. The child life specialist I told you about."

Fiona could immediately see who Gabe got his striking tidewater blue eyes from. High cheekbones, a layered bob with long swoopy bangs, and a ready smile put Fiona at ease. She extended her hand. "It's a pleasure to meet you, Fiona. Gabe has told us so much about you."

Behind his mother, Gabe's eyes widened. He mouthed that that wasn't true, and Fiona almost laughed. "It's a pleasure to meet you, Mrs. Cavenaugh."

"Call me Vicky." She looped her arm in Fiona's. "Come on. I want to introduce you to everyone else. Gabe, grab those burgers on your way out."

They passed through a pristine white dining room with one dusty blue accent wall and mixed chairs at the table. French doors led to a patio in the backyard. As soon as Fiona stepped out, all conversation ceased and attention turned in her direction.

"Everyone, this Fiona. She's the child life specialist Gabe's been shadowing." She turned to Fiona. "And this motley crew is Gabe's family minus his older brother who's on duty and couldn't come."

Vicky then took her to each person and introduced them one by one. Fiona met Gabe's father, Joe, who was as tall and as bald as his son. She met his two sisters, Ellen and Sadie. Ellen, who was several inches taller than Sadie, was obviously in her last trimester. She was married to Michael White. Sadie, like Gabe, was single.

Gabe's sister-in-law, Maria, had a slight Cuban accent, long legs, and a gorgeous smile. Since his brother Chip was at work, Maria was managing their two sons by herself but the boys were too busy playing to come meet the new lady. Fiona forgot their names as soon as she heard them because she was trying to figure out what kind of duty Gabe's brother would be on. She wanted to ask, but everyone assumed she already knew.

Vicky asked Fiona to excuse her because she still needed to get some food ready. She promised she'd come back to talk more, but refused Fiona's offer to help. "You just sit down and relax. I know how hard you must work." Fiona found a spot and sat down, watching the family interact.

Gabe came up and handed Fiona a glass of lemonade. "You okay? I didn't mean to desert you." He sat down in one of the padded chairs across from her. "Information overload?"

"Not too bad, but don't quiz me on everyone's name or history." She pressed a hand to her growling stomach. The smell of the grilling meat was making her hungry. She glanced at the table where Ellen was sitting. "I didn't know your sister was expecting. Are you excited to be an uncle again?"

"It's hard to be an uncle. You can only be a cool uncle when they're little. When they get to be teenagers and you act like you care, you're just creepy."

Fiona laughed. "I've never thought about it like that."

"Isn't it true? Didn't you feel like that with your uncles?"

She froze, but quickly reminded herself that she didn't have to bare her soul to these people. She was there to help her kids. That was all. "No," she said, "I didn't have an uncle."

"Well, I guess you were lucky. Chip's boys are fun to be with.

Maybe I'll teach them how to fish. Chip hates fishing, so if they're going to learn, it'll have to be from me or my dad." He turned to watch the two little boys wrestling in the grass. "But I think I'll wait until they're a little older."

"Good call." Fiona sipped her tea. "You said Chip was on duty. What does he do?"

"He works for the Pinellas County Sheriff's Department. He's a detective, and his real name is Joseph like my dad's. He's a 'chip' off the old block."

As a child, Fiona's interaction with the sheriff hadn't been the best, but in her work at Bryce Memorial, she'd met many officers she'd come to appreciate. "Is he often gone from your family events?"

"More than me." Gabe grinned and stood. He held out his hand to her. "Come on. It looks like Dad's got the burgers grilled, and I'm starving."

"Now, there's a surprise." She pretended she didn't see the hand he offered to help her stand.

The family squeezed in on benches around the long table. Gabe indicated that Fiona should take the seat next to him. Before they ate, the whole family joined hands, and Gabe's father prayed. It seemed as natural to them as breathing.

And it was the kind of family Fiona had always dreamed of.

She forced a quivery smile as they began to pass the food. Vicky was apparently used to her son's appetite and had prepared a mounded bowl of potato salad and large pot of baked beans. The hamburgers, now topped with thick slices of cheese and rashers of bacon, stood stacked like bricks on the platter. Fiona's cheeks burned. Her watermelon salad seemed miniscule in comparison to the selections offered.

Gabe heaped potato salad onto his plate, exclaiming his mother's was the best, but his sister Ellen chastened him to leave some for the rest of them. Fiona chuckled. At least she wasn't the only one to give Gabe a hard time about his massive caloric consumption.

"This is delicious." Sadie held up a piece of watermelon. "I love the mint. It's new, Mom, right?"

"Fiona made it." Vicky gave Fiona a welcoming smile. "And it was sweet of her to bring it."

The family chatted for the rest of the meal, occasionally asking Fiona questions but not prying. She enjoyed seeing the easy camaraderie the family experienced, but it also made her heart ache. What would it have been like to live in a family like this her your whole life?

She knew coming here would trigger a lot of feelings, so she imagined them trickling through her fingers like the sand yesterday—grief, anger, sadness, provision. The last thought stopped her. She wasn't being fair. God had provided for her when it was most needed and she'd be forever grateful.

"Are you all right?" Gabe whispered in her ear. "I know we're a lot to take in, but you haven't even finished your burger."

"I'm fine. Just thinking too much." She took a bite, and he went back to attacking his own private buffet. She chuckled. Baldy could sure eat.

Soon the picnic was over and Vicky commandeered her while she directed Gabe and his father to do the cleanup. Both men jokingly balked and motioned for the women to relax. Vicky led Fiona inside to the living room, where they made themselves comfortable.

Vicky didn't wait long to start with her questions. Although she apologized, she admitted she found this new program fascinating. "When I was a pediatric nurse, we didn't have anything like this."

Fiona said a prayer and leaned back into the cushions. She would answer everything as honestly as humanly possible. She didn't want to give Vicky any reason for not trusting her.

"So." The air conditioner hummed, and Vicky pulled a blanket over her legs. "Tell me everything. Where did you go to school? How many hospitals have child life programs? Why is it important?"

"They call me Mary Poppins or the play-lady, but that's only the surface of what I do." The answers then rushed from Fiona like a tidal wave. Even though she tried to keep her passion in check, she couldn't keep the excitement from her voice when she shared some of the stories of ways her work had made a difference. Vicky was dumbstruck by the fact that with Fiona's help, doctors and radiologists could do medical tests and procedures without sedating the patients most of the time.

"I can help kids know what to expect. I tell them what they'll hear, smell, taste, and feel. Adults know what to expect when an alcohol swab is opened. They know the strong smell that will follow. Children don't." Fiona drew in a deep breath to force herself to slow down. "We play-practice the procedures beforehand and the child gets to 'teach' the doll or stuffed animal how to relax and cope."

"So why Mary Poppins?"

"I have a whole bag full of tricks."

Vicky grinned when Fiona told her about the ever-present

I Spy book, Playdoh, bubble wand, hippy stick, and light-spinner that she used to distract young children during procedures. "I can see you're passionate, and I can see the program's value to patients and their families, but I'm guessing my son wants to know how you justify the cost."

There it was. Gabe had told her.

"The American Academy of Pediatrics has come out saying that child life programs are an important component of pediatric hospital-based care. There are more than four hundred child life programs in North America, and every children's hospital in the nation has a child life program. It's a benchmark for integrated patient- and family-centered care. We know that kids who interact with a child life specialist need less sedation, have shorter hospital stays, and leave better adjusted, but there's just not enough data yet to evaluate the cost-effectiveness of child life services." Fiona released a long slow sigh. "But you and I both know it's hard to put a dollars and cents value on psychosocial needs."

Vicky leaned forward, her hands clasped together. "I don't envy my son, Fiona. You make a great argument for your cause. I can see its value because I've been in the trenches, but it's going to be an uphill fight to convince the number crunchers your program is vital."

"I know." Vicky had spoken so gently that hot tears filled Fiona's eyes. "But I can't give up. I'm fighting for my kids."

Vicky covered Fiona's hand with her own. "I'll do what I can to help, but it's ultimately in God's hands."

"And Gabe's," Fiona whispered.

"Honey, he's got quite an ego, but even he knows he isn't

God." She looked up. "And look who's here?"

"I came to rescue Fiona." Gabe placed his hand on the back of the chair. "You've interrogated her long enough, Mom, and it's time for dessert. Homemade ice cream."

Fiona stood. "I really should be going."

"No ice cream?" Gabe made it sound like she was committing a crime. "Are you sure?"

Fiona nodded. "Thank you for a wonderful evening, but I'd better be going."

Gabe motioned to the door. "Then I'll walk you out."

She started to tell him there was no need, but he raised his palms in a surrendering gesture. "See, what I have to put up with, Mom?"

Vicky drew close and put her hand on Gabe's back. "Son, you're in trouble. I heard that they call her Mary Poppins, and you know what that say about Mary Poppins. She's 'practically perfect in every way.'"

Fiona's cheeks warmed as she thanked the woman again for her hospitality.

Gabe followed her out the front door and down the walk. "My mom liked you."

"She's a wonderful lady. You're very lucky." Fiona touched the button to unlock her car door and opened it.

Gabe remained on the curb. "So, how did your job interview go yesterday?"

Fiona turned. "What?"

"You said you had an appointment but it wasn't at this hospital. If you're going to be hired at a new hospital, I figured that would make this decision easier for everyone."

Anger burst inside her chest like a flare. Didn't he realize how hard it was for her to come tonight? Had he not learned anything about her? "You think I'd leave my kids and my program just like that! I know we haven't known each other long, but I thought you'd have already figured out that much about me. The only reason I came tonight was to fight for my program. That's who I am. I will not abandon those kids. You got that?"

Gabe jerked his head back.

She hopped into her Kia and slammed the door, leaving Gabe gaping in her wake. Once the engine started, she peeled away before the tears began to flow.

CHAPTER 7

Running his hand over his smooth scalp, Gabe stared after Fiona's Kia. What had just happened? Why had she gone off like a nuclear bomb? Maybe she was a nutcase after all.

He pounded up the walk and paused at the door. He looked back over his shoulder at where her car had been and shook his head. The evening had gone so well, and none of this made sense. Still, it should not be getting to him like this. He should simply let it go, but he couldn't. What was it about Fiona that made him care?

He needed to end this whole charade as soon as possible. He already knew what he was going to have to tell the board, so on Monday he'd tell her he had to recommend the Child Life Program be terminated. End of story. Sure, she helped the kids, but in the end, it was the only financially responsible decision he could make. Then, he could get back to doing the work for which he'd been hired.

Relieved to have made a decision, he squared his shoulders and entered the house.

"There you are." His mother looked up from the living room couch and gave him a proud, maternal smile. She patted the seat next to her, so he plopped down. "Gabe, that is a delightful, passionate young woman, and you have to save her Child Life Program."

Gabe moaned. Now, his mom was on her side. "Mom, the hospital can't afford—"

"Your hospital can't afford not to. I can assure you that

St. Joseph's Children's Hospital in Tampa has child life specialists, and I remember reading that the National Hockey League's Tampa Bay Lightning team funded a child life playroom at Tampa General."

"You think the Clearwater High School's Tornadoes will fund the program since we're fresh out of national teams?" He could feel the sarcasm dripping from his voice.

Undeterred, his mom pressed on. "Fiona said the American Academy of Pediatrics recommends child life services in hospitals, too. It appears it's become an expected part of giving today's patients and their families quality care." She took his hand. "Besides, I have faith in you. I know you can find a way to save this program."

He leaned his head back on the couch cushion, closed his eyes, and scrubbed his face with his hand. It was all so much more complicated than his mother understood. William Case had already made up his mind, and where was he supposed to find this magical money? Mr. Case might have made it sound like it was Gabe's decision, but he knew from experience that Mr. Case did not like his positions on matters questioned. Could disagreeing with Mr. Case cost him his job?

He should have known better than to ask Fiona to come over tonight. His soft-hearted mother wouldn't be able to resist stories about hurting children. Good grief. Even he'd been moved in the last few days, but the truth of it was, the child life program might be a nice dessert, but it wasn't a main course.

Now, he was not only letting wacky Fiona down, but he was also disappointing his mother. Like the hamburgers on the grill, he was cooked.

Fiona slid into the pew beside her foster mother, Cathy Martin. She glanced down the row. Cathy and her husband Duane, who were in their late fifties, had added another foster child to their present family of four. She was a teenage girl and Fiona could only imagine what the girl was thinking and feeling on this first Sunday with the Martins at a church service.

She hoped the girl would come to allow the Great Physician to heal her hurts. Only God could be the perfect parent.

Cathy, who Fiona called Mom Cat, draped an arm around Fiona's shoulders. God was the perfect parent, but Cathy came in a close second. Unfortunately, Fiona had blown through two other foster homes before finding a forever home with the Martins. It wasn't the fault of those other foster parents. They'd been okay people, but at the age of twelve, Fiona was a scared, confused, and grieving girl who was angry with the world and impossible to live with.

But Mom Cat was different. Fiona had felt it from day one, and Mom Cat refused to stop loving the angry girl, no matter how bad she got. Fiona laughed because she had gotten pretty bad.

Fiona found herself singing the songs, taking communion, and listening to the sermon but not truly focusing on any of it as she should have. Her mind kept going to the new girl in the family at the end of the pew.

By now, Cathy and Duane would have told her the family motto "Families aren't like socks. They don't have to match to go together." It was a silly saying but it seemed to set the stage for life in the Martin home. Every child that came in would become part of a loving, mismatched family, and each child brought their personal trauma along with their teddy bear and a garbage bag of their clothes.

After the closing prayer, she turned to Mom Cat and embraced her. "I'm sorry I didn't call this week."

The older woman studied her face. "What's wrong? I can see it in your eyes."

"Can we talk later?" She nodded toward the new girl. "Are you going to introduce me?"

Mom Cat followed Duane and her clan—a fifteen-year-old girl, ten-year-old twin boys, and the new girl—into the aisle. She turned to the newest addition. "Talia, this is Fiona. She's one of our girls. Fiona, this is Talia."

Talia wore a red t-shirt which set off her honey-bronze skin. Her caramel colored eyes were set in a stubborn, don't-you-dare-talk-to-me stare. Fiona guessed the girl probably had a beautiful smile, but doubted she'd see it today. "Hi, Talia. It's nice to meet you."

Mom Cat smiled at her new daughter. "Talia came last week. We got her enrolled at New Hope on Friday, and she starts on Monday. She's in the ninth grade."

"It can't be easy to switch schools, but you'll like New Hope Christian, and it doesn't hurt that Mom Cat teaches fifth grade there. If you need something, she'll be close by." Fiona offered a reassuring smile, but Talia didn't respond. Despite all of her training with children, this girl was a hard one to reach.

"Can you join us for dinner, Fi?" Duane asked. "Cathy made pot roast."

They looked so hopeful, Fiona couldn't refuse. "You know that's my favorite."

Half an hour later, juicy pot roast, potatoes, carrots, and gravy filled the Martins' dinner table. All the kids except for Talia had had a part in getting the table set. Fiona pitched in, too, but Talia sat in the living room alone until it was time to eat. When everything was in place, she finally joined them at the table.

When the family joined hands to pray before the meal, Talia kept her arms tightly crossed. Fiona remembered being much the same when she first arrived. She didn't want to like this family, even though it was hard not to, because liking them felt like she was betraying her own family.

Mom Cat would give Talia space for a few more days, then she'd share the family's expectations and give her household responsibilities. She was probably sharing a room with fifteen-year-old Solana, which might help, too. In time, Cathy and Duane's consistent lifestyle and unconditional kindness would help Talia adjust. If Fiona had to guess, Talia's life had been one upheaval after another.

Fiona glanced at Talia's plate. It was nearly as full as Gabe's would have been. Could that skinny teenager possibly eat all that?

Fiona looked at Mom Cat, who shook her head, telling Fi to say nothing. Fi knew from experience that many foster children had food issues because of past neglect. Was that part of Talia's story?

When dinner was over and the dishes cleared, Fi offered to help Mom Cat finish up. The kitchen hadn't changed much since Fiona had graduated from high school so she knew where everything was kept. It was a far cry from the kitchen she'd been in yesterday at Gabe's parents'. While that one sported pristine white cabinets and floors, this kitchen had scuffed cabinet doors and scorched pots.

Fiona dipped her hands into the warm, sudsy water and began to scour the roaster.

"So, are you going to tell me what's been going on?" Mom Cat picked up a dish towel. "I knew even before I saw you today because you'd gone dark on me."

She set the roaster in the dish rack. "Dark?"

"Incommunicado. And you only push me away when you're hurting. You always have." Mom Cat began to dry the pan. "What's wrong?"

As Fiona washed a few more things that wouldn't fit in the dishwasher, she began to explain the events of the last week. She held nothing back. It was cathartic in so many ways.

Mom Cat laughed at some parts of the narrative and teared up at others, but she never interrupted. After Fiona shook the bubbles off her hands, she picked up a towel.

"Fi." Mom Cat put the dishwasher detergent tab in and started the machine. "I hope you know I am incredibly proud of you and all that you've done."

"But I don't know if I can do this. What if I'm not enough to convince Baldy to keep this program?"

"First of all, let me recommend you don't call him Baldy. Second, God put you here for a reason. You need to trust that." She moved to the window and looked out to the backyard where the twins, Trevor and Tristan, were shooting hoops. "The boys are going home next week."

Concern knifed through Fiona. "What? Why? Mom, I'm so sorry."

Mom Cat smiled. "Don't be sorry. It's a good thing. Reunification is our goal because every child wants to be with their bio mother, and she's doing great. She finished treatment six months ago, and she's stayed clean."

"But you'll miss them so much."

"I will, but they were never mine to keep." She squeezed Fiona's arm. "Unlike some of you."

Fiona's heart warmed, but her concern for the boys hadn't ebbed. "What about school? Will they have to change mid-year?"

"Now, there's a story." She sat down at the table and waited for Fiona to claim the seat across from her. "Their mother applied for a scholarship to New Hope and she got it. It takes care of the remainder of this school year."

"Mom, you and I both know scholarship dollars are pretty scarce in the middle of the year."

Mom Cat grinned. "But they can happen—with a little help."

"You and Dad are paying for the boys?"

"No, we don't have that kind of money, but a certain brother of yours, who owns a terrific mechanic shop, may have seen the need."

"Ambrose?" Fiona blew out a breath through pursed lips. "Wow. I know he's changed, but—well—just wow."

Ambrose had been sixteen when Fiona came to live with the Martins. He treated her and her little sister like annoying kids most of the time, but he'd teased and played ball with them occasionally. Over time, he'd become the kind of big brother of which Fiona had always dreamt.

But outside of the house, Ambrose was a different person. He was a risk-taker. His Greek heritage, with his dark eyebrows and long lashes, made him popular with the ladies, too. After he'd barely graduated from high school, he left the Martins' home and got in with the wrong crowd. A short stint in jail had taught him his current profession, and when he got out, Mom Cat and Duane helped him find a place to work.

A sweet chuckle came from Mom Cat. "You look dumbstruck."

"I am. I knew he purchased the shop for himself when the owner retired, but I never thought that cocky Ambrose would fund not one, but two scholarships at New Hope. Do you remember how much he said he hated that place?"

"I guess he's maturing. He's not looking at things with the same eyes that he used to." Mom Cat turned her attention to the girls in the living room. "Speaking of eyes, you're the one with the vision to see what kids need. Why don't you take a stab at getting Talia to open up?"

"What's her story?"

"I could tell you what it says on paper, but you know that's never the whole story. When she's ready, she'll tell us." Mom Cat wrapped an arm around Fiona. "But I have a feeling this girl is going to need you. I hope you're up for it."

Sometimes Mom Cat believed in Fiona more than Fiona believed in herself. Sure, Fiona sensed Talia's fears and pain, but she was no therapist. "I don't really know how to help her."

Mom Cat smiled. "You'll think of something."

Fiona scratched her head. What could she use? Maybe she could get both Talia and Solana to play a game, but what one? She walked into the living room and squatted down in front of the shelf containing the games. Monopoly? Too long. The Game of Life? Too unrealistic for a foster kid. Battleship? Only for two.

Pie Face? No way on earth.

She stood up and frowned, then remembered she'd purchased a game yesterday to use at the hospital for teens. "I'm going to run out to my car and get a game we can all play together."

After unlocking the car, she retrieved a shopping bag from her trunk and hurried back inside. She cajoled both Duane and Talia to join Solana and Mom around the coffee table.

When Fiona pulled the 5 Second Rule game from the bag, Solana squealed. "I played this at my friend's house. It's so much fun. I loved it!"

Talia did not look impressed, but Fiona didn't let it deter her. She slit the cellophane wrapping on the game and pulled it off. Static electricity made the awful stuff cling to her hand. Solana laughed and helped her ball up the wrapping. Fiona then tugged off the game's lid and began to set up the pieces. She held up the first piece. "This is the five-second timer and these are the cards. After a card is read, we flip the timer over and you have five seconds to give the answers. Let's try one together." She selected a card and held it in one hand. In the other, she held the timer. "Okay, here's the question. Name three Chinese meals. Go." She turned over the timer.

"Moo Goo Gai Pan," Mom Cat said.

Solana clapped her hands. "Sweet and sour chicken."

Fiona glanced at Duane. He shrugged. He'd never been a Chinese food fan.

"Lo mein," Talia mumbled.

"Yes! We did it!" Maria held up her hand for a fist bump, but Talia didn't move.

Fiona chuckled. "Hey, don't leave her hanging."

Rolling her eyes, Talia lifted her fist, and in a half-hearted effort, completed the action.

Fiona felt the familiar satisfaction she got when she first got through to difficult kids. It was a start, and for that she'd be thankful.

They went around the circle completing the cards. Name three breeds of dogs. Name three brands of cereal. Name three sports where jumping is involved. They soon discovered five seconds was not very long.

"Okay." Mom Cat picked up a card. "This one is definitely for Fiona." She handed the timer to Solana and snickered. "Ready? Okay, name three famous bald persons."

Fiona stared. Only one face came to her mind. Come on. Think. She pumped her fists up and down. "Caillou, Elmer Fudd, and, and—"

"Ding!" Solana called.

"And Charlie Brown!"

"Too late." Mom Cat hiked a shoulder, then gave her a knowing look. "Maybe you should have given us a not so famous bald person's name."

Talia leaned forward and picked up the timer. "And maybe you should watch something other than cartoons."

Fiona laughed and saw a flicker of a smile on Talia's lips. The Martin family magic was working. They weren't socks. They didn't have to match. And God was tucking Talia into Fiona's heart.

What would Gabe think of this ragtag group she called family? It didn't matter. He was never going to know about them. In fact, she doubted he'd ever speak to her again.

CHAPTER 8

Stepping into the hall from a patient's room, Fiona looked toward the entrance doors to pediatrics. Still no sign of Gabe. It was already past nine. If he were coming, he'd have been here, and if he couldn't, he'd have sent word. It meant one thing. She'd blown the whole deal on Saturday night.

She made her way down the hall to the playroom, which was staffed by volunteers she'd trained. No medical procedures or medical discussions were allowed in the playroom. The area was devoted totally to playing.

"Hi, Georgia." Fiona sat down on one of the lime green children's chairs. A retired school teacher, Georgia loved kids and understood them well. Today, she was wearing an apple red sweatshirt with "Happiness is Being A Grandma" written across the front.

Fiona glanced around the familiar room. When she'd first come to Bryce Memorial, she'd painted a mural of colorful swirls like unicorn breath on a cold morning. With Ambrose's help, she'd built a castle wall in one corner where kids could read, and painted it with faux bricks. There was a craft area, a toy area, and movie and game area. There was even an air hockey table for the teens. What would happen to all this if her program was cut?

"Fi? Is something on your mind?" Georgia left the child she was reading to and came over and sat down in a rocking chair.

"No, I was just checking on you. Any problems?"

Georgia laughed. "No doctor would dare breach the walls of

the playroom with you on duty."

"Or you." Fiona dropped the wooden pieces of a puzzle in their proper place. Once completed, a sweet panda stared back at her. She set the puzzle aside. "I'll let you get back to Elise."

"Oh, I think she's fine. There are only so many times a body can be expected to read the same book."

"*The Goose Egg*?"

"By Liz Wong. Yessiree. I read it four times already today. The girl loves elephants."

"I could give you a break and read to her."

"Or you could tell me what's troubling you. I'm a good listener."

Fiona swallowed. She promised not to put up a fuss among the staff, but surely she could tell Georgia. She was a volunteer, after all. "The hospital is considering cutting the Child Life Department."

The older lady huffed. "Why on earth would they do that?"

"Budget deficit." Fiona closed her eyes and felt the prick of tears behind the lids.

"Are you going to fight it? This is the best thing there is for these kids."

"Thank you, Georgia. I'm doing my best to find a way to save it."

"How are you going to do that? Are you going above someone's head? To the board of directors? Or maybe the press?"

"I'm sorry. None of that, and I shouldn't have mentioned it. I just wanted you to know I won't give up easily."

"I'm sure you won't. I believe in you." Georgia made a shooing motion. "Now, you go do your thing, and I'll do mine even if it's reading that book again. If I could spend twenty-five years with second graders, I doubt that *The Goose Egg* will send me round the bend."

"Maybe you could suggest a craft. Elephant ears out of paper plates?" Fiona grinned and stood.

"Thanks. She'll love it." Georgia slowly pushed out of the chair. "Go on now, and don't worry about a thing."

Fiona left the playroom wishing she could follow Georgia's advice and not worry. Instead, she seemed to have a list of things deserving her concern. The Bible verse about not being anxious about anything, but praying about everything came to mind. Great. Now, she was worrying about worrying.

Patients kept her busy the rest of the morning, but after noon, her pager went off. She was needed in the ER. She hurried toward the exit doors of pediatrics.

"Fiona." The clerk held up a paper. "I forgot to give you this when you came in."

Fiona grabbed the message, stuffed it in the pocket of her khakis, and made a beeline for her office to grab her purple bag and medical doll.

A mahogany skinned nurse named Leticia, with a broad smile and even broader hips, met her as soon as she entered the Emergency Department. She recalled Leticia telling her that her name meant happiness, and Fiona thought the name fit perfectly.

Leticia led her to the patient's room. "We've got an asthmatic four-year-old who needs a breathing treatment but he's frightened of the mask. He's not in immediate danger now, and it's his first attack, so it scared his poor dad to death. I knew you could help getting him off to a good start and help calm him down."

"I'll do my best." She put her hand under the antibacterial foam dispenser and caught a whiff of alcohol as she rubbed her hands together. She pushed open the door and found a wheezing little boy sitting on his father's lap inside the treatment room. The boy looked familiar. Had he been here before?

She squatted down in front of him. "Hi, Anton. I'm Fiona. I'm a child life specialist." The father cocked his head to side with a quizzical look on his face. Maybe he'd never heard of Child Life.

"My job is to be your friend while you're here. Hospitals can be scary places, but I'm going to help you know what's going on." She held up the doll. "We're going to play doctor, okay? You can make this guy all better."

The boy scowled. "Dolls are for girls."

"But this guy isn't a doll. He's a sick boy like you, and he needs you to be his doctor." Fiona pulled up a stool and sat the doll on her lap. "Are you ready to help him?"

Fiona withdrew a child-sized oxygen mask from her bag. The manufacturers had designed it to look like a fish with eyes above the nose piece and fins out to the side, but Anton shrunk back from it.

"Our little guy here is having trouble breathing, so he needs to get some medicine. He needs you to put the mask on him like this." She demonstrated by holding the mask to the doll's face and pulling the elastic cord around the back. "You want to try?"

Anton reached out slowly and examined the mask. She wasn't surprised that he put the mask on himself first. He then pulled it back off and slipped it on the doll. "This will make you all better."

Fiona smiled. "Dr. Anton, can you tell him that the nurse will put medicine in this tube?" She indicated the medicine cup below the mask. "And that he needs to leave the mask on until all the medicine is gone."

Anton repeated most of what she'd told him.

"And one more thing, Dr. Anton. Please tell him that it doesn't hurt at all. All he needs to do is breathe."

"It doesn't hurt. Just bweeve." Anton told the doll, then he looked at his dad. The muscular man nodded his approval.

"When the nurse turns on the machine, it'll make a noise like this." She hit the button on the nebulizer and let it hum for a few moments. "I'm sure your patient will be feeling better soon, Dr. Anton." She laid the doll on the bed. "Nurse Leticia, I think Anton is ready for his breathing treatment. Right, doctor?"

He nodded and Leticia held up the mask. Fiona was glad to see that Anton didn't shrink back against his dad, but sat up ready to begin. The small patient watched as Leticia added the ampule of medication to the cup.

"That's medicine." Anton told his dad.

Leticia allowed Anton to put the elastic band around his head while she adjusted the mask. "I'm going to turn on the machine now. Remember, it will hum."

"And I bweeve." Anton's words were muffled.

Fiona rustled through her bag and located her *Big Seek-And-Find* book. It was like the *I Spy* one but easier for toddlers to master. "Since it's going to take a little while, would you and your dad like to play with my book?" She opened the first page. "Let's see. What's the first thing we should look for?"

The book kept Anton entertained until the breathing treatment was complete. After Leticia removed his mask, Fiona stood up. "Anton, it was nice to meet you."

"But I met you before, Feewona."

"Here at the hospital?"

"No, at Whammy's."

She tilted her head to the side in confusion.

"That's what he calls his Grammy. I'm Chip Cavenaugh. I believe you were at my parent's house the other night. You work with Gabe, don't you?"

She nodded.

He extended his hand. "Thank you for your help today. You worked wonders."

Fiona hurried from the room and leaned against the tile wall outside the door. Cavenaugh? She should have guessed Chip was related to Gabe. Other than the fact that Chip had a full head of hair and Gabe did not, they looked similar. Tall, lean, athletic build. And Anton? He had seemed familiar, but she'd not spent much time with the children that night.

She sucked in a deep breath. There was no doubt about it. Anton was Gabe's nephew, but did Gabe know his nephew was here? He'd want to be informed, but her hands were tied. Because of HIPPA laws, she couldn't tell him his nephew was in the ER.

Rubbing the kink at the back of his neck with his hand, Gabe looked across the desk at the hospital's chief operations officer, Manny Medina.

Manny held his hands as if he were praying and brought them to his lips. "I simply don't understand why the idea of cutting the Child Life Department wasn't run through me first. I shouldn't have to hear about something this significant from upset staff members."

Gabe's stomach knotted. The graying COO with a nose the size of Texas was right. It was part of the chief operating officer's job to encourage patient and physician satisfaction and make sure the hospital was providing quality services. Hadn't Case mentioned the possible need to cut Child Life to the COO? As the chief financial officer, Case met with the COO and the CEO all the time. He should have told them what he was considering weeks ago. Still, Gabe didn't dare make this Case's fault. Blaming him would only come back to haunt Gabe.

"I'm sorry, Manny. There's been no formal decision or recommendation made to the board. It's something we're considering. That's all." Gabe leaned back in his chair and forced himself to look calm. He liked Manny. He and Manny had even played golf a few times, and he didn't want to make an enemy of the man. He was normally easy-going, but was fiercely protective of the hospital and its staff. "By the way, how did you get wind of this possibility? From Miss McGrath?"

"No." Manny picked up a pen and tapped it on the surface of his desk. "There's a volunteer in the pediatric playroom named Georgia. She called me this morning."

"A volunteer?"

"Georgia is my son's godmother." Manny met Gabe's gaze. "And a family friend."

But how would Georgia know? There was only one source. She had marmalade hair, and apparently, a big mouth.

"Manny, if we have to cut something, wouldn't you agree that Child Life would be one of the easiest to live without? I'll admit it does serve our youngest patients, but they won't die without it."

"It's very popular with the patients and staff, and if we want to be competitive with the other hospitals, we have to offer quality services. Some say Fiona McGrath is a miracle worker."

The knot in Gabe's stomach tightened. "I'm afraid the money might just not be there. I wish it were."

The older man stood and waited for Gabe to follow suit. "I won't fight you on this, but I hope you'll consider looking for another option."

"I'm already doing that, sir." Gabe extended his hand. "And again, I apologize for not coming to you first."

"You're young, Gabe, but you're doing a good job. Better than Case ever has. You actually care. I have faith you'll find a solution to this that works for everyone."

"I certainly hope so."

Manny had no idea how much Gabe meant that. Between Fiona and his mom, the last thing he wanted to do was cut this program. But numbers were numbers, and it made him sick to think that in the end, he'd still have to recommend that the Child Life Program be terminated.

He walked out of the room and glanced at his watch. Lunchtime. But in a rare occurrence, he wasn't the least bit hungry.

CHAPTER 9

Fiona sat on the edge of ten-year-old Garrett's bed with a controller in her hand. "Take that, Gare-Bear!" She watched the spaceship on the screen explode.

Garrett retaliated by taking out two of her ships. He threw his arms in the air. "I won! I beat you!" He wiggled in the bed, doing a celebration dance. Unfortunately, the cast on his leg prevented any real dancing.

"You sure did." Fiona clicked a few buttons, then set the controller on the stand. "But now I switched it so you can play against the computer without me. Can I come back later for a rematch if I have time?"

"You'd better hurry. I'm going home tomorrow." Garrett beamed. "The physical therapy guy said I'm the best he's ever seen on crutches."

"That's what I heard. But why hurry home? Are you tired of us already?"

"Nah, but I miss my dog."

"Well, if I don't see you again, give him a big hug from me." Fiona turned toward the door.

"Hey, Fi, what's the joke of the day?"

Fiona smiled. She'd almost forgotten. "Why did the teddy bear say no to dessert?"

"Why?"

"Because he was stuffed."

Even though this was the tenth time she'd shared the joke of the day, Garrett had an infectious, bubbly giggle and Fiona found herself laughing all the way out of the room. Too bad Gabe wasn't here to meet Garrett. She imagined Garret was his kind of boy—fun and rambunctious with good self-esteem. They would have had a lot of fun with the video game. Maybe Gabe would have also noticed how important it was to do normalizing activities with children of all ages. Kids, even in the hospital, had to be kids.

Gabe seemed to be making himself quite scarce today. She wondered if his brother had contacted him about his nephew's asthma attack. As far as she knew, Gabe might still have no idea about the event.

Even though it was time to head home and she was exhausted, she had a game she wanted to make for a three-year-old. The little boy wasn't handling the trauma of being in the hospital well. Since he'd been admitted during the night, he'd become non-verbal, and Fiona needed to get him talking again. She could tell he understood what everyone was saying, but not speaking was his way of having some control over a situation that was not making him happy.

She'd spent a while with the little boy's mother and learned that he liked animal crackers and was a big fan of Curious George.

After feeding Buttons and cleaning the Flophouse, she rummaged through a shelf full of odd items and located the small plastic basket she wanted. She also collected all the plastic fruit she had on hand. Now, if she could just figure out how to make the basket into a monkey, she could make something she hoped would help get her patient to start talking again. An idea came into her mind.

She sat down at her computer and made a quick search.

Within seconds, the printer popped out a photo of a monkey. She cut out the monkey and a plate-sized circle from a piece of poster board. Once she glued the monkey onto the circle, all that would be left was to cut the monkey's mouth open and attach the circle to the basket with ribbons. The search through her desk drawer yielded a new X-Acto knife. The one Gabe had used to cut the urinals had been discarded.

She located her cutting mat, set it on the table, and placed the monkey picture on top. She held the picture circle in place with her left hand and put firm, but steady, pressure on the knife with her right. She carefully cut around the monkey's lower lip.

A knock on the door caused her to jerk. The blade sliced across the tip of her index finger on her left hand. Blood immediately squirted from the cut. She gasped and reached for a tissue to put pressure on the wound and keep the blood from dripping on the monkey face. Through clenched teeth, she managed to tell the person at the door to come in.

Gabe stepped inside. "Oh, good. You're still here. I was hoping…" He eyed her hand. "Fiona, you're bleeding."

"And here I thought your only superpower was invisibility."

"What?"

She rolled her eyes and grimaced. "Remember, I didn't see you all day. You vanished."

"We can talk about that later." He spotted the X-Acto knife on the table and reached for her hand. "Good grief, Fiona. Did you do it with that? Let me see the damage."

"You're a numbers guy. What are you going to do? Count to three and make it all better?"

"Fiona." His tone was low and serious.

"Gabe." She imitated the sound, but held out her hand. The scent of his cologne—a fresh, woody, oriental fragrance—reached her nose as he drew closer.

He gently peeled back a corner of the tissue. It began to bleed again. "You need stitches."

"Actually, I need a job, but you're trying to take that away." She saw the look of frustration on his face, and relented. "Sorry. I just need a decent bandage. I'll be fine."

He passed her a couple more tissues from the box. "Okay. Hang on. I'll be right back. Keep pressure on it."

No. Duh. Like she didn't know that. She pressed hard on the wound, but the cut throbbed to no end. She summoned her coping skills. Breathe deep. In. One. Two. Hold. Three. Four. Out. Five Six. This should be working, but all she could smell was the lingering scent of his cologne. It was unnerving.

Gabe burst back in with a familiar nurse from pediatrics in tow. Middle-aged Penny had on a *Green Eggs and Ham* scrub top.

"Gabe, I asked for a bandage."

"And he brought that and more." Penny sat down beside her. "Don't be too hard on him. They're so cute when they're worried. Let's take a look." Penny examined the digit and announced that it did indeed need stitches. She pulled out a roll of gauze and made quick work of wrapping the wound. Penny looked from her to Gabe and feigned deep concern. "Do you want a wheelchair to take you down?"

"No, I thought I'd take my scooter." She eyed the contraption by the door. "But I'm not very good at steering it one-handed, so watch out."

"Are you out of your mind?" Gabe ran his hand over his bald

head. "You are not driving—that."

Fiona laughed. It felt good even if it made her finger throb harder. He was so predictable but, she had to admit, concerned Gabe was adorable.

"Why don't you take her down?" Penny gave Fiona a knowing sideways glance. "Then, if she faints, you can catch her."

His forehead crunched with concern.

"I won't faint." Fiona wiggled the fingers on her right hand. "And I have five other fingers on the other hand with which to press the elevator buttons. I think I can handle this alone."

"But you won't have to because you've got a personal escort. Come on." Gabe took her arm and helped her stand. They took a couple steps toward the door, then he paused and turned to her with a massive grin on his face. "Should I get your purple bag? I've learned a lot, and you might need a distraction."

She gave him a warning look of annoyance, but the flutter in her chest annoyed her even more. She couldn't tell him, but Gabe Cavenaugh was more than enough of a distraction.

Gabe paced back and forth in the ER's treatment room. Why was it taking so long for someone to see to Fiona?

She sat in a hard plastic chair holding her bandaged hand. "Will you sit down? This is not an emergency."

"They should be in here by now."

Fiona tried to explain—again—how patients were triaged and her little cut would be pretty low on the list. In fact, now that the bleeding had stopped, she admitted she was seriously considering going back upstairs and Super Gluing the wound shut.

Didn't she realize he wasn't going to let that happen? Not on his watch.

She shifted in her chair and cleared her throat. "So, why did you skip out on me today?"

He stopped mid-stride. "Didn't you get my message? I called up to pediatrics and asked them to tell you I got called in to the COO's office."

Her brow scrunched. "You did? Is everything all right?"

"It would be if you didn't go around spouting off your woes to every volunteer in the hospital." He emphasized the point by using both hands.

"Excuse me? What are you talking about?"

His stomach growled. He'd missed lunch and now it was nearly supper. "You told some volunteer named Georgia about the possibility of your program being cut. She happens to be the godmother of the COO's son. She called him as soon as you left."

"And?"

He dropped into the chair beside her. "He's upset because he had no idea we were considering this."

"But he's the chief of operations."

"I thought my boss had already discussed it with him. He's not happy."

"I'm sorry, Gabe." She released a long breath. "I didn't mean to break my promise to you, but I needed to talk to somebody."

"I know, and I'm sorry. This is an impossible situation." He leaned his head back against the wall. "Later in the day, Case wanted to talk to me. Numbers are just not adding up, and pretty soon the day was gone. I didn't mean to vanish on you." His stomach protested more loudly than it had before. "I didn't even get lunch."

"Then, you can go home. I'll be fine."

He glared at her. Why couldn't she understand he had no intention of abandoning her? And where was the doctor?

"Okay, at least go down to the cafeteria and grab something to eat. You can even get it to go and bring it back here. It could be a while yet." She smiled. It was a genuine, no snark, no walls smile, and it touched him in a way he wasn't expecting. Fiona was special and vulnerable, and he wanted to take care of her.

Wow. His blood sugar must be bottoming out. He stood. "I think I will go get some food. Want anything? A sandwich?"

She held up her bandaged hand. "I don't think I can manage that."

"I'll find you something." He walked to the door and paused. "Are you sure about this?"

"Your stomach is growling so loud it's making me hungry, so yes, I'm sure."

She looked so alone and small sitting in that room, he almost changed his mind. But those feelings were dangerous and if he didn't leave now, he might regret it forever.

He'd purchased two footlong club sandwiches, chips, and cookies for himself, and chicken fingers, fries and a brownie for Fiona. Surely she could eat that one-handed. But when he entered her treatment room, she was nowhere to be found. He set the bag of food he'd smuggled in by the chair, went into the hall, and flagged down a nurse. "I'm looking for Fiona McGrath. Did she leave?"

"Fi? Mary Poppins? Oh, they needed her in three."

"What?" he growled. "She's not on duty. She's a patient."

The nurse glanced toward the treatment room where Gabe guessed Fiona had been taken. "Mister, I promise you that the teenage girl in three needed her more than Fi needed her finger stitched. Bad accident. Why don't you go to the waiting room? I'll tell her nurse to come get you when they're ready to fix her up."

Transfixed, Gabe stood in the hall for a moment, debating what to do. Fiona shouldn't be working. He could demand to see her, but that wouldn't do any good. He could go home, but he couldn't bring himself to do that either. A rumble in his stomach reminded him of his most pressing need.

He grabbed the bag with the grub and took it out to the waiting room. Gray padded chairs lined the walls of the room. A lighted acrylic art panel with engraved swirls made a noble attempt at brightening the space. The carpet, at least, was made up of colorful blocks of gray and yellow. How different it was to be on this side of the hospital—the patient's side.

Most of the chairs were occupied, but he found a spot in the corner near an end table. He could have gone down to his office, but he'd told the nurse he'd be out here. Still, if Fiona was well enough to help in an emergency, she could most likely make her own way home.

He pulled out his sandwich. For some reason, he couldn't leave her. He didn't know why, but he couldn't do it.

An hour and half later, he'd polished off both sandwiches, the chips, the cookies, and Fiona's food. Still, there was no word of her. He'd asked several times, but had received the same answer. The child life specialist was helping with a patient.

He pseudo-read the *Time* magazine beside him and used his cell phone to peruse through his emails. His phone rang, and he was surprised to see it was Chip. He answered it. "Hey, what's up?"

"Did Fiona tell you I saw her today?" Chip asked from his end of the line.

"No. Where?"

"In your Emergency Department. Anton had an asthma attack."

"Is he okay?"

"He is now. They fixed him right up. Gabe, your Fiona was amazing."

"She's not my Fiona." Irritation nudged him. Why hadn't she said anything?

"Well, she did an incredible job with Anton. I was impressed."

Great. One more person to add to the Fiona Fan Club. "How's Anton now?"

"He's doing fine, but it was pretty scary. We had no idea he had asthma. We'll have to see his pediatrician this week." He paused. "I was glad it happened when I was at home. I took Anton, and Maria stayed home with Amador. I just wanted to let you know he was doing okay now."

"Give Anton a hug from his Uncle Gabe. Thanks for calling."

Gabe stared at his phone, his pulse hammering. Had Fiona been paying him back for ditching her today by keeping Anton's visit a secret? He scrubbed his face with his palms. *Calm down and think about this.* Fiona was all about supporting the child and the family. She had to have her reason. What was it?

The answer hit him so hard he sucked in a breath. HIPAA. The Health Information Portability and Accountability Act. Of course, she couldn't say anything. He didn't have a lot of contact with the HIPAA policies, but he'd attended mandatory training, and he recalled the rules on who could share what medical information as being very strict.

He heard a swish and looked up to see her coming out of the Emergency Department doors. Her finger had a fresh bandage on it, and her face was ashen. He swallowed hard. What had they done to her?

She stopped when she saw him and a faint smile formed on her lips. Blood, now dried brown, streaked her ivy green shirt. Couldn't they have least given her a scrub shirt to wear? He crossed the waiting room in four long strides. "You okay?"

She nodded. "You didn't have to wait, but I'm glad you did."

Heat pooled in his chest. "Come on. Let's get you home."

"I can't go home." She wrapped her arms around herself. "The girl is in surgery now, but she might need me later."

"You need to at least eat, right?" He wouldn't argue with her at this moment, but he had no intention of letting her return later.

Was she cold? He shrugged out of his jacket and draped it around her shoulders.

She pulled it close and thanked him. "I guess I look pretty scary."

He placed his hand on her back and directed her toward the parking lot. He might not be able to save her program, but at least tonight, he could be there for her in some small way.

CHAPTER 10

The street lights whizzed by in streaks of colors. Fiona leaned back against the passenger seat in Gabe's car and closed her eyes, content to let him make the decisions for the moment.

She pulled the lapels of his jacket more closely around her and drank in the scent of his fresh, woodsy cologne. The man did smell good. She closed her eyes and drifted off.

"No!" Her own voice woke her. How could she have called out here?

Gabe put his hand on her arm. "What's wrong? You okay?"

"Sorry. Bad dream." How could she admit it was more than a dream? It was a recurring nightmare, and one she'd survived years ago. She noticed they were pulling up to the Olde Bay Café in Dunedin. It was a perfect choice and she was starving. "Wow, I slept all the way here?"

Gabe parked the Mazda. "Yep. Hope you like fish. I didn't want to wake you up to ask."

"I do, but I think I'll skip the peel-and-eat shrimp." She held up her bandaged hand.

"Probably a good idea." He reached in his back seat and passed her a Florida Gators hoodie. "I thought you might want to put this on over your shirt."

"Embarrassed to be seen with the bride of Frankenstein?"

"No, I—"

"Gabe, thanks." She took the sweatshirt and gave his suit jacket back to him. "And thank you for letting me use your coat, too."

He draped it over his arm. "Come on. Let's eat."

They climbed out of the car and Fiona was assaulted by the fish smell of the marina mixed with the aromas of the restaurant's cooking. She carefully managed the hoodie over her injured finger, slid the rest over her head, and tugged it in place. The sleeves hung a good four inches below the tips of her fingers. She pushed up one side with her good hand, but frowned at the other long sleeve.

"Here, let me." Gabe gingerly pushed the sleeve upwards.

He'd never been so close to her before. His blue eyes were tender tonight. She noticed the well-groomed dark stubble on his jawline and, for a moment, she ached to reached up and touch it.

He stepped back and quickly put his jacket on. "You look good in Gator blue."

"I'm just glad you don't have an orange hoodie. It might clash with my hair."

He chuckled and motioned toward the rear of the café. They found a seat outside beneath an umbrella-covered table looking over the marina.

The last time Fiona had been there, it was summer and the sun had been setting about this time. Since it was now winter, the lights sparkled off the glassy water and lit the masts of the boats. She stared out at the ebony water. The steady cadence of the ocean gently lapping against the dock begged her to relax.

An effervescent young waitress with a bouncy ponytail took their orders and brought their soft drinks. She wasn't surprised when Gabe added an appetizer to their order, but was a bit shocked when he picked the most expensive appetizer on the menu—Walt's Crab Cakes.

Gabe asked Fiona about what he'd missed during the day. Grateful he hadn't inquired about the teenage girl she'd been with in the ER, Fiona told him each of the patients she'd seen, but skipped Anton. Worry tightened her stomach. Did he know about his nephew?

The waitress set down the crab cakes along with plates for the appetizer. Gabe put one of the plates in front of her and then took one for himself.

With her good hand, she smoothed the napkin over her lap.

"Fi, I noticed you pray before you eat and so do I. It's been quite a day. Do you mind if we pray together?"

She slowly nodded her approval. God was good and He was providing for her. She needed this right now.

He held out his hand, palm turned upwards, and she gently placed her unbandaged hand in his.

The only words she could have used to describe his prayer were "genuine" and "humble." Honestly, it was so different than the confident, almost arrogant man she dealt with daily.

He paused before going on. "And Lord, please take care of my nephew. I'm grateful Fiona was there for him today."

He knew. Tears filled her eyes, and she swallowed as he ended the prayer. She needed to get herself under control. If she were on the Starship Enterprise, she would have ordered "Shields up." Tears over an asthma attack? Sure, it had been a long day, but this was ridiculous.

The crab cake cut easily with her fork, and the citrusy Dijonaise topping only made it more delicious. She hadn't realized how hungry she was until she'd taken the first bite. Gabe had better eat his crab cake fast before she devoured it, too.

A few minutes later, her grouper taco arrived loaded with coleslaw, key lime vinaigrette, and avocado. Gabe had chosen the pricey sea scallop dinner and a basket of chips. At least he'd added fresh fruit. How did the man stay looking so healthy? She had to admit the mango vinaigrette drizzle covering his scallops smelled amazing.

She maneuvered the taco into her right hand and took a bite. "So you know about Anton. I'm sorry I couldn't tell you. I wanted to, but—"

"But you couldn't because of HIPAA laws. I know." He cut into a scallop. "My brother said you were great."

"Your nephew is adorable."

Gabe met her eyes. "Fiona, I meant it when I said that I was glad you were there."

She didn't know how to respond to that. "Like you always say, anyone could do it."

Her words jabbed him and she could see it in his eyes. They needed to move on to a safer subject. She asked about what Gabe did when he wasn't in the hospital and learned he was an avid cyclist. Gabe told her that he and his brother went on twenty-five- or thirty-mile rides at least twice a week.

"It's a good way to stay in shape." He speared his last bite of scallop. "How's your taco?"

"Great. I just don't have your speed-eating ability."

"It takes practice." He grinned. "Give it time."

A spark shot through her and she tamped it. He hadn't meant that comment the way it sounded. The waitress stopped over, and he asked about dessert. They had three choices: key lime pie, apple crisp pie, and peanut butter pie.

"What's your poison?" He raised his eyebrows.

"If I could eat another bite, which I can't, I'd pick the peanut butter."

"Peanut butter it is. Two forks, please."

"Gabe." She tried to sound serious.

"Hey, I'm sure I can take care of your half if I have to."

"Probably very true, Captain High Metabolism."

They chatted throughout the rest of dinner and, to her surprise, she managed to eat some of the dessert. The waitress brought the check and she reached for her purse to pay her share.

"No." Gabe grabbed the check folder. "I've got this. It's the least I can do to say thank you."

When they left the restaurant, she started for the car, but Gabe put his hand on her back and steered her toward the beach walk.

"I should get back."

"Not yet."

Their footsteps thudded on the wood slats of the pier, the tide crashing beneath them. "Fiona, what happened after I left?"

Tears welled in her eyes and she attempted to blink them away. "A teenage girl was in a bad car accident. They called me in to help with her."

He leaned against the wooden rail. "And?"

She stopped beside him. "She ended up needing surgery."

Turning towards her, he seemed to study her face. "There's more, Fiona. I know it. You were really upset when you came out of the ER. Why did this one get to you?"

She glanced at her watch. The girl would be out of surgery by now. "I really should get back."

"No." His voice was calm but firm. "I'm not taking you there."

He wouldn't do that. Would he? "Gabe, this girl needs me."

"There are nurses there. She'll be fine."

"You don't understand." She raised her voice. "I know how scared she is. I know what it's like to have all these people doing things to you, but not knowing what's going on. Someone needs to walk with her through this."

"How do you know?" His brows scrunched and his gaze bore into hers.

"Because."

"Because of what, Fiona?" he demanded. "What drives you to do this job?"

"It's none of your business." She started to walk away.

He took hold of her arm. "Don't hide. You know it is my business. If you want me to believe in you and your program, then I need to know why it's so important to you."

She whirled on him. "You can't handle knowing. You live in a perfect world with a perfect family, but not all of us have been so lucky. Why do I know what that girl is going through? Because I was that girl. Only I was twelve and my mother died in the same accident that night."

He dropped his hand as if he'd been burned. "I'm so sorry."

"It gets worse." She glared at him. "She committed suicide by driving the car intentionally into a concrete barrier on the interstate. I was a passenger in the car." Tears rolled down her cheeks like rain on a windowpane. "I was badly injured. At the hospital, everyone was rushing around. They did test after test. I remember the strange smells and sounds like it was yesterday. Nobody would tell me what was going on, and I was so scared. I just wanted to know about my mother."

His Adam's apple bobbed up and down and his chest heaved. "How badly were you hurt?"

"Internal bleeding and a concussion." She swiped at the tears with her good hand. "They took me to surgery and put me under without explaining a thing. I woke up so angry and confused. My head felt like it would explode. Finally, they sent in a chaplain who told me my mother had died. Just like that. She was gone. My sister and I were alone. Abandoned."

He pulled out a handkerchief and passed it to her. After a few minutes, he asked, "Why wasn't your sister with you in the car? Was she with your dad?"

She gave a wry laugh. "My dad was in prison. That's what sent my mom into such a depression. My sister was at a friend's house. She blames me for not stopping my mom that night. She said if she had been there, she could have saved her."

"You know that's not true, right?"

"No, I don't know. In fact, she's probably right. She could always get through to Mom when she was in one of her moods. I couldn't. I always disappointed my mom. Too much like my dad, I guess." She wrapped her arms around herself to ward off the growing chill of the night air and swallowed the lump in her throat. She turned to look at the dark waters below. "There you have it, Gabe; the reason why I know the Child Life Department is vital. You've heard my whole ugly story. Are you happy?"

"Your pain certainly doesn't make me happy." His voice caught on the words. "I wish with all my heart that I could take it all away."

"But you can't." She took several deep breaths, trying to stem the tears. "Can I go back now and check on that girl? You can drop me off, and then head home. My car is at the hospital, and I'll be fine."

"I'll take you back, but I'm not going anywhere." He cupped a warm hand around her cheek and turned her face toward his. "You can't scare me away, Fiona McGrath. Want it or not, I'm here to stay."

She covered his hand with her own and drank in the compassion in his eyes. Want it or not? She did want it. She wanted to seek refuge in the comfort of his arms and let him hold her until all the awful memories washed out to sea.

But that wasn't for someone like her.

She lowered her hand and stepped away. She wasn't enough to save her mother, she wasn't enough to save her program, and she certainly wasn't enough for an All-American guy like Gabe.

CHAPTER 11

Gabe pulled his Mazda to a stop in the hospital parking lot, and Fiona had her seatbelt off before he could turn off the car's engine.

"Wait up." He climbed out of the car and met her on the sidewalk.

"You don't need to come in."

He breezed past her and started toward the hospital. "The deal was one week. As far as I can tell, I still owe you two days plus a few extra hours because I cut out early."

She hurried to meet his long strides. "But this patient is dealing with a very difficult situation. It's going to be rough. It's not what I had in mind."

He ignored her and took the steps two at time. Deep in his soul, he knew he was doing the right thing. He'd prayed all the way from the restaurant to the hospital. What else was he going to do? Fiona had become silent and withdrawn. He didn't blame her, and God could do more to give her peace than his words could.

Their exchange had been emotional, and her story tore at him even now. What kind of a mother would do that with her child in the car? And what kind of guilt was Fiona carrying even today? It wasn't fair.

He held the hospital door open for her, then followed her down the hall. Since it was so late, the halls were nearly empty. His steps squeaked on the newly polished floors. The floor polish freshened the usual antiseptic smell of the hospital. The sweetness seemed like a strange contrast to the painful bitterness they were facing tonight.

They stepped off the elevator and made their way to the ICU where she swiped her identification card and the doors swung open. She stopped in the open doorway and turned to him. "For the last time, I want you to know that you really don't have to, nor do you want to go with me."

He crossed his arms over his chest. "If you're going, then so am I."

Fiona straightened her shoulders. "Gabe, this teenager lost her leg tonight."

His Adam's apple bobbed. It suddenly felt like a glob of peanut butter had lodged in his throat. "I understand," he managed to say. "But I'm not leaving."

"Suit yourself." She stopped at the desk to get the room number and to ascertain her patient's condition. They nurse relayed that Alexis Hunley was stable but still sedated. When she reached the girl's room, she knocked softly, then eased the door open.

Gabe didn't want to intrude, so he stood just inside the door and watched the scene before him. Lights in this ICU room had been dimmed, and a woman he guessed to be Alexis's mother was sitting on a small couch that he believed could be made into a bed. A monitor emitted a faint, steady beep next to the patient's bed.

White blankets were pulled up to the girl's shoulders, and it appeared her injured leg was propped on a pillow. This teenager, whose biggest worry had probably been boys a few hours ago, now faced a life without a limb. She was a pretty girl with long, dark brown hair splayed across the pillow. Had the girl's mother brushed it? It seemed like something his own mother would do for one of his sisters.

Fiona moved past the teen sleeping in the bed and stood in front of the girl's mother. "Hello, Mrs. Hunley. I'm the child life specialist Fiona McGrath," she spoke quietly. "I was with Alexis in the ER before they took her to surgery. Do you mind if I sit down so we can talk?"

The young mother patted the space beside her. "They took Lexi to surgery before I got to talk to her. I came as soon as they called, but I wasn't here soon enough. Did she know what had happened?"

Fiona nodded. "She did, and I tried to make sure she understood what was going on around her."

The mother dabbed at her eyes. "Was she scared?"

"I did my best to help ease her fears. That's part of my job—to walk with her and with you through this whole situation. She showed remarkable courage, but I'm sure she was still afraid." Fiona twisted on the couch, tucked her left foot behind her right knee, and cradled her injured finger in her lap. "Tell me about Alexis."

"She just got her license two months ago. She's a junior in high school. I shouldn't have gotten her that car. Everyone knows a red car is just asking for trouble."

Fiona didn't attempt to address the guilt the woman was dealing with. Instead, she laid a hand on the mother's arm. "What is Alexis like?"

"She knows what she wants in life. She's smart, driven, and has a great sense of humor, but she's a big risk-taker. She's the cheerleader that's called a 'flyer.' You know, the one at the top of the stunt. She has even had some colleges approach her to cheer at their schools." Mrs. Hunley covered her mouth with her hand.

"She can't be a cheerleader anymore, can she?"

"Probably not." Fiona handed the mother a fresh tissue from a box on the table.

The mother dabbed at her eyes. "She'll be devastated."

"But all those things you said about her, like that she's smart, driven, and has a great sense of humor, will help her discover her new self. And you said she's a risk-taker, right? That will make a world of difference, too." Fiona inhaled a slow breath. "I know all this is difficult and strange, so let's talk about what you can expect to happen next here at the hospital."

From his place by the door, Gabe recalled the three P's and recognized this as preparation.

Fiona explained that tomorrow when Alexis woke up, she would see a host of hospital personnel. The surgeon would be in, but so would physical therapy, occupational therapy, and someone from psychiatry to see how Alexis was coping. "She'll have a whole team taking care of her. I'll come in early in the morning to talk with Alexis about what to expect during the day. Knowledge will really help her cope."

"How can a teenager possibly cope with losing her leg? No more dances. No more sports. Can she even drive? The doctor said she was lucky because it was a below the knee amputation. Tell me. What is lucky about any of this?"

"She's alive." Fiona placed her hand on the mother's arm. "I know there are a lot of unknowns and you have every right to be concerned, but with your help, she'll get through this and so will you."

"What will the kids at school say?"

"If you like, I can go to her school and talk to her classmates and friends about how they can support her both now and when she returns, but we can discuss that with her later. Is there anyone who can come stay with you here tonight? I can call them for you."

"No, my husband stayed home with our son. My sister will be here in a few hours so my husband can come join me."

"Good. You need support, too. And rest." Fiona glanced at Gabe, then turned back to Mrs. Hunley. "Are there any other questions I can answer?"

"No, I can't think of any right now." She stood and Fiona followed suit.

"If you think of something, here's my card." She pressed it into the woman's outstretched hand. "Call and I'll come anytime—day or night."

"I could use one thing." Mrs. Hunley looked from her daughter to Fiona.

"What?"

"A hug."

Fiona drew the woman into her arms and let the woman sob.

Gabe slipped from the room, his heart aching for this family and for Fiona. It was so much easier to manage columns of figures if you didn't put faces and stories with them. Not only did Fiona love her job, she knew she made a difference. She'd turned his whole preconceived notion about Child Life upside down.

If he hung around Fiona much longer, would she turn his life upside down as well? He could leave right now. She didn't expect him to stay, and they'd simply remain colleagues. It was for the best.

He started for the elevator and stopped when he saw a feather on the waiting room's carpet. How odd? He picked it up and studied the streaked blue, black, and brown plumage. "Hope is a thing with feathers." He whispered the words that Emily Dickinson had once penned. "That perches in the soul."

"And sings the tune without the words, and never stops at all." Fiona stood in the doorway, her silhouette backlit by the lights in the hallway, her hair glowing. "It's one of my favorite pieces. Just like the birds need feathers to fly, we need hope." She stepped into the hallway. "I wanted to give that to Mrs. Hunley tonight."

"Maybe this was meant for her and Alexis." He passed Fiona the feather. "I found it here in the hall."

Fiona stared at his outstretched hand where the feather rested. Was she so tired she couldn't process what he'd said?

She shook her head slowly. "No, I don't think it was for them."

He blinked. She seemed a little disoriented again, and his instinct to protect her kicked in. "Fiona, can I give you a ride home?"

She gave him a sweet smile. "No, thank you. I have my own car, and I think I'd rather be alone. Good night, Gabe."

When she walked away, he let her. She was like a bird. If he held her too tightly, he feared he'd crush her wings, and there'd be no greater crime than to crush Fiona McGrath.

CHAPTER 12

Mindful of her injured finger, Fiona eased the lid off a pint of chocolate Häagen-Dazs. With only one hand, it wouldn't be easy to indulge in her favorite comfort food, but she'd manage somehow. After all, ice cream would eventually melt, and she could drink it like a shake if she had to, right?

She curled up on the couch, drew a soft blanket over her legs, and picked up the remote. A little reality television diversion might accompany the ice cream perfectly. With the push of a button, familiar faces filled the television screen. She was secretly rooting for Ally, but thought Mindy would be an okay choice, too, but not that nasty, troublemaker Talullah.

The ice cream had softened enough that scooping it one-handed was relatively easy. The first bite melted on her tongue. She loved ice cream way too much. It was almost sinful. Almost. But she personally thought God must have been smiling when man discovered ice cream.

She considered calling Mom Cat to tell her about the day, but rehashing it would be a torment of its own. Why had she told Gabe everything? Now, she'd have to face him tomorrow, and even if he didn't ask any more questions, it would hang between them like a beacon pointing out her inadequacies. It might even give him more cause to axe Child Life. After all, it proved his earliest observation, and he now knew the wacky director of Child Life had an even wackier mother.

A knock on the door startled her but, given that her apartment had a security system, she knew it had to be a neighbor. She made her way to the door and peeked through the keyhole. To her surprise, it was her foster brother, Ambrose. After slipping the chain from the door, she opened it wide. "What's wrong? Is everything okay with Mom and Dad?"

"Everything's fine. Can't a guy just visit his little sis?" Ambrose flopped down on the couch. "Having a little chocolate therapy?"

"The best kind." She went to the freezer and pulled out another pint. She tossed it to him and followed it with a spoon. She then took the chair beside him.

Ambrose eyed her hand. "Hey, what happened to your finger? Some kid finally bite you?"

"Funny." She rolled her eyes. "I cut it with an X-Acto knife at work and had to get stitches. So, Ambrose, tell me why you're really here."

He ripped off the top of container of ice cream. "I ran into your sister today. Your real sister."

"Shannon?"

His brow scrunched. "Do you have any others?"

"I might have. Maybe my dad had more secrets than the ones that came out at his trial." Her voice had a sarcastic edge. "So how was Shannon?"

"Bad." He took a giant bite and spoke with his mouth full. "She's using again."

A rock dropped in Fiona's stomach. "Did she come to you for money?"

"Worse." He stuffed an enormous spoonful in his mouth, but still managed to say, "She wanted your address."

"Please tell me you didn't give it to her." She fidgeted with the fringe on the blanket.

He shook his head. "I know better than that. I told her that once she was checked into a rehab to let me know and I'd relay it to you. But then I got to thinking. She knows where you work. I wanted you to be warned in case she shows up there."

She rubbed the back of her neck with her good hand. "Could this day get any worse?"

"What's going on?" Ambrose propped his feet on her coffee table. "Mom told me about the problem with your department. Did they make a decision?"

"No, not yet." She covered her lap with the blanket. "It was just a horrendous day in so many ways, but I'll be okay, and if Shannon shows up, I'll handle it."

"You don't have to do it alone. That's why I'm here. Call me if she tries to get a hold of you." Ambrose polished off the last of the ice cream and set it on the coffee table. "Fiona, I'm serious. She's unpredictable when she's using. Your mom really did a number on her."

"On both of us, you mean. Shannon still blames me for our mom's death."

"Well, Daddy's girl should have blamed him." Ambrose stood up. "His choices destroyed your family, but healing from the trauma is her responsibility."

Fiona followed him to the door. He wrapped her in a bear hug. "God's got this, Fi."

The words touched her, especially coming from Ambrose and his new relationship with the Lord. How many nights had she lain awake praying that Ambrose would come to know Jesus? What had it been? A little over a year since he was baptized?

He pulled away. "Now, lock your door after I go."

"How'd you get in anyway?"

He chuckled. "Some nice lady upstairs believed my sob story about forgetting my key and let me in."

She punched his arm. "That's awful."

"Awful dangerous." He grinned, displaying a mouthful of white teeth. "You should bring that up at your next apartment meeting."

She shut the door behind him and secured the locks and chain, before returning to the couch and her melted ice cream. When she picked it up, her hand was shaking so badly she didn't dare try to finish it. Her heart began to palpitate and a cold sweat broke out over her body. Her breath came in short gasps and she clawed at her neck needing more air. Her stomach roiled.

It's a panic attack. Panic attacks are not going to kill you. Instead of fighting the feelings, she tried to visualize the attack as a wave she was riding until it came ashore. *You might feel like you're drowning, but you know how to swim.* She grasped the container of ice cream and held it until the cold penetrated her feelings. She practiced the full body breathing she knew so well and, as soon as she could, she opened her iPad and began to play Candy Crush. The same distraction she used on children worked on herself. After about ten minutes, the sensations began to dissipate.

She couldn't blame her body for the attack. It was fighting and doing exactly what it was supposed to do when threatened. The only problem was it had been misled. The danger wasn't physical, it was emotional, and she hadn't had a panic attack in several months.

It was time for this day to end. Exhausted, she climbed into her bed and cuddled with the softest blanket she owned. Before she could say "amen" to her prayer, she'd fallen asleep.

CHAPTER 13

Honk! Honk! The sound of a car horn shook Fiona from her dreams. She jolted upright and looked at her clock. Nine o'clock. She moaned. How had she overslept?

She vaulted from the bed and grabbed a pair of dark brown pants and a pale blue blouse. She could easily manage the blouse with the bandaged finger. The hair, on the other hand, might be a challenge. With no time to shower, she gave her hair a spritz with a water bottle and pulled her curls back with a polka dotted headband. She skipped makeup, grabbed a protein bar, and was out the door. She glanced at her watch. Not bad. Fifteen minutes from pillow to parking lot.

A car pulled up beside her. "Want a lift?"

She turned and looked at the driver of the familiar red car. "Gabe. What are you doing here?"

"I was concerned when you didn't come in. You had a rough day yesterday." He motioned to the passenger door. "Hop in."

She smiled and kept walking. "I can drive my own car."

He inched forward. "But does your car stop at IHOP?"

"Gabe, I have to get to work."

"Okay then, we'll pass on pancakes. But you can at least let me drive you to work since I came all this way."

She rolled her eyes. "All fifteen miles. Wow, I bet that was taxing."

He made a pouty face, so she took pity on him. She walked around to his passenger side, climbed in, and secured the seatbelt.

"I can only imagine what the peds nurses are thinking."

"I covered for you. I said you worked all evening, and needed to sleep in." He pulled out onto the street. "I even checked on all your kiddos, except for Alexis."

Fiona's hand shot to her mouth. "I was supposed to be in there for her early."

"I called the ICU nurse and she said they were leaving her mostly sedated for the morning. You'll still be able to talk to her before everyone arrives." He stopped at a red light and turned to her. "You doing all right today? Finger hurt?"

"Dull ache, and thank you for taking care of all that." She fiddled with the bandage on her finger. "Did you notice if any of the kids were going to have procedures today?"

"Penny said there were a couple of x-rays, but no big tests, and the broken-leg boy is being dismissed." He made another turn. "Easy day for us, right?"

The way he said "us" seemed so casual and normal it warmed her. In fact, she found all of his efforts this morning endearing. But why the big change? Was he trying to be nice before dropping the other shoe? Or worse, was this pity caring? Like he'd heard her family story and now he needed to be nice to the poor foster kid? She glanced over at him and he smiled back, but she saw the truth in his eyes. Pity.

"Gabe, listen, you don't have to treat me any differently today than you did before. Sure, yesterday was a bad one, but I'm not fragile. I can handle it."

"I'm not—"

"Not intentionally." Since he'd pulled into the hospital's parking lot, she waited until he'd stopped the car to finish the conversation. "Let me make something clear. I didn't have the perfect family and, in many ways, I got dealt a bad hand in life. Not all of us are dealt the right cards, but that doesn't mean I can't reshuffle the deck and pray for a better outcome."

"Is that what you did?"

"It's what I'm trying to do every day." She unbuckled her seatbelt. "So, no more Poor Fiona eyes. Got that?"

"Yes, ma'am." He made a mock salute. "But for the record, the concern was genuine. I really do care."

"I believe you." She fingered a loose thread on the hem of her tunic. "But you're still going to have to cut my program, right?"

He didn't answer.

She flashed him a smile and swung the door open. "Well, I've got today and tomorrow to change your mind, so let's get a move on. Time's a wasting."

As Gabe had expected, Fiona's first stop was to see Alexis and her family in ICU However, she found that Alexis had been moved to post critical care down the hall. They found the room and knocked before entering.

Gabe remained by the door, but Fiona stood beside Alexis's bed and introduced herself. The teenage girl still wore a nasal canula, and a large bandage swathed her head. Bruises and scrapes mottled her face as well. Gabe could only imagine how horrendous that car accident had been. Alexis appeared to still be under the influence of medication, which he imagined was quite necessary.

From his place by the door, he couldn't hear the initial questions that Fiona asked, but Alexis seemed to connect with her immediately. She raised the head of her bed and nodded. Fiona explained that Alexis could expect a lot of people in her room today. She told the young woman how physical therapy would be in to help her with stretching and strengthening. They also discussed the kind of emotional support she could expect.

"There are some excellent videos on YouTube by amputees. They've been where you are. Do you want to see one?"

Alexis did, but her mother wasn't so sure. She feared it would upset her daughter.

"I understand what you're saying, Mrs. Hunley, but remember being informed is a way of being in charge of your own care. Alexis needs information and she needs to know she's not alone, but we can always address this later if that's what you two want."

"Honey, are you sure?" Mrs. Hunley squeezed her daughter's hand.

"I am, Mom."

"Then, let's watch them together."

Fiona nodded and pulled out an iPad and opened a video. She propped the iPad on the tray table. "This is a young woman's vlog of her own below-the-knee amputation. Within a year, she was back driving, riding a bicycle, swimming, dancing, and skiing, but it's different for everyone. Press Play when you're ready."

Fiona watched along with Alexis and her mother. When the video ended, Alexis asked if she could borrow the iPad and watch some more.

"Of course." Fiona smiled. "I'll stop by later and see if I can answer any questions. And remember, you can call me if you have any questions or want to talk."

In the hall, Gabe followed Fiona to the nurses desk. "She seems to be handling it well."

"I think she's in shock, but seeing someone her age who's gone through the same thing and is doing well will give her hope." Fiona typed information into the computer, then turned to him at last. "Lunch?"

"Need you ask?"

Even though he felt like he was devouring his meal, Fiona was finished long before him. Finally, she looked at her watch and announced that they needed to hurry. Two o'clock was Pottery Time.

Gabe grabbed a fistful of cookies and followed her out of the cafeteria. "What's Pottery Time?"

"Time to make pottery." She shook her head in mock disbelief. "Really, Gabe, that should have been obvious."

He scowled at her.

"I have a small pottery wheel upstairs. I let the kids that I call my 'frequent flyers' work with the clay. They're the kids who have chemo and other diseases that land them in the hospital often. They need a little extra care."

"But don't you have to have a kiln or something to fire the things they make?"

"I have a friend with a shop. And to be honest, most of the kids' creations don't make it that far. They just like to play with the clay. In fact, the youngest patients just get air dry clay."

Fiona explained that everything they needed to transform the pediatric playroom into a pottery studio was kept in an art closet. He followed her into the room and paused to take in the sight. He'd never been in this particular room and the bright colors, collection of toys, and piles of books made him wish he were a child again.

"Can you help me set this up?" Fiona dragged a six-foot white resin table from the closet with her good hand.

He crossed the room in three long strides. "Give that to me and watch your finger." He extended the table's legs and flipped it over onto the tiled area of the room. "Now what?"

She draped it with a vinyl tablecloth and tugged the elasticized corners in place. "Can you pull the pottery wheel out? It rolls."

He asked her where she'd like it to go. After she indicated the spot, he rolled it over and locked the wheels, so it wouldn't move while the children were working, before plugging it in. Fiona went to the closet and withdrew a pile of aprons. She put on the clay-splattered brown one and passed Gabe a fresh blue striped one. Fiona fumbled with the waist ties, her bandage making the tying difficult.

"Here, let me." He nudged her hands out of the way and took the strings in his own.

She untucked her massive orange curls from the neck strap. "I hope you can make a better bow on my apron than you did on the vases."

"You mean the urinals you tried to pass off as vases." He pulled the loops taut and eyed her shapely figure. "Perfect, if I do say so myself. Now what?"

"We have to get the clay ready." She set a brick of clay wrapped in cellophane on the table. "Have you ever worked with clay?"

He tilted his head to the right, his brows scrunching. "Does kindergarten count?"

She chuckled, opened the clay, and began to knead the dough one-handed. "What did you make in kindergarten?"

"A royal mess." He pointed to her pile of clay. "Can I do that for you?"

"Sure." She stepped out of the way. "It needs to be softened. It's more of a push and roll motion than classic bread kneading."

He did as she'd said, pushing the clay away from him and rolling it over. "I know this is going to surprise you, but I actually do knead bread. Bread making is one of my fortes."

"You know a claim like that will have to be backed up with proof, don't you?" She took a sterile glove from a box in the closet and carefully eased it over her bandaged finger, then tugged it into place. She wiggled her digits in the air. "There. That should work. I'm going to go get a pitcher of water, so we can get started."

"Where are the kids?"

"Don't worry," she called over her shoulder. "They'll come."

She walked out of the room with a little bounce in her step. Mentally, Gabe called it the Pottery Day Prance, and he loved it.

The clay in his hands became pliable. If he had any idea of what to do, he might give the pottery wheel a spin before Fiona returned, but with his luck, he'd give the term "throwing pottery" a whole new meaning.

Two children, obviously chemo patients, entered the playroom, escorted by their mothers. They bounded over to his table and looked up at him with eager faces. He swallowed, his pulse doing the quickstep. What was he going to do with them?

"I wanna make a bowl." A girl in pink pajamas announced. Her thinning hair was nearly the same color as Fiona's.

"No, me first." The boy next to her announced. "I done this

before, so I know what I'm doing."

"Whoa." Gabe leaned close to them. "I'm afraid you both have to wait for Fiona to come back."

"I love Fiona. She's the bestest." The girl spun in a circle.

"If you're with Fiona, that makes you Shrek." The boy snickered at his cleverness. "I'm going to call you Shrek all day long. Shrek. Shrek. Shrrrrek."

Fiona breezed back into the playroom with a pitcher of water in hand. "Simeon, it's not nice to call people names, even fun ones like Shrek."

"He's bald like Shrek." The boy rubbed his own bald head.

"But he's not green." Fiona poured the water into a pink hospital washbasin before dropping a small sponge in.

Simeon crossed his arms in front of his body. "You sure he doesn't burp like Shrek?"

"Simeon, enough." His mother took hold of his shoulders and turned to Gabe. "I'm sorry. He gets carried away. Simeon, why don't you read some books while Megan goes first?"

He frowned, his lower lip jutting out. "Why does she get to go first?"

"Because she knows how to be polite." His mother gave him a stern, no nonsense look, and he finally stomped away.

Fiona beckoned Megan to the pottery wheel and put a plate on it. She referred to the plate as a bat. The bat, she said, could be removed with each person's finished product and a new one put on. She also demonstrated how the pedal worked. After she dampened the wheel with her hand, she gave the seven-year-old a marble-sized ball of clay and told her to make an "x" across the center of the wheel. "That will hold your clay in place." When Megan had finished, Fiona slammed a ball of clay the size of an orange on the center of the "x." She pushed down on it to make sure it was secure.

Gabe pulled up a chair so he could watch everything. He noticed that Fiona had moved the foot pedal so that she could be the one to control the wheel's speed and not Megan. She pressed the pedal and the wheel begin to slowly spin.

"Now, just dribble some water from the sponge on it like this." Fiona dripped a little from the sponge, then passed the sponge to Megan. "There are two rules with using the potter wheel. Keep it wet and keep it spinning. Yes, that's it!"

She then explained that it was time to center the clay. She had Megan dampen her hands in the pink basin, then put her wet hands around the clay. "Go ahead and squeeze it hard."

The clay formed a pillar. "Look, it's growing!" Megan pulled her hands away. "Now, can I make a bowl?"

"We sure can try." Fiona dampened her own hands and Megan followed suit. Fiona pressed down on the column Megan had created and made a mound again. "Okay, watch this." With a wet thumb, Fiona made an indention in the center of the clay. "That's going to become the center of your bowl."

"Can I do it?" Megan bounced on her toes.

"You sure can." Fiona directed the girl's fingers as they made a center in the bowl. Soon the bowl began to take shape. "Let's add some water." She gave Megan the sponge to drip a little moisture on her creation. "Shall we make it fancier?"

Megan nodded.

"Get your hands wet again and then hold them gently around the outside of the bowl. That's it." While Megan followed Fiona's directions, Fiona put one finger a half inch from the bowl's top and soon a rim formed.

"How did you do that?" Megan eyes were wide.

"We did it together." Fiona told the girl she could take her hands away because the bowl was perfect. Fiona removed the bat and set the bowl aside. "I'll take this to my friend's shop. She'll put in in a special oven called a kiln that gets to eighteen hundred degrees. When we have Pottery Day next time, you can paint it."

Fiona repeated the procedure with three more children, including Simeon. Gabe was transfixed. No matter how poorly a child listened or if they messed up, she never raised her voice. She laughed with them and all left with a brilliant smile on their sick little faces.

She glanced at the clock. "We have time for one more."

He looked around. "I'm afraid that you're fresh out of kids."

"I'm looking at a big one, right now." She flashed him a grin and pushed her hair out of her eyes with the back of her hand. "Think you can handle the pottery wheel."

"This is not a win-win for me. If I say no, I'm a wimp because four kids just did it. If I say yes, then I'm most likely going to end up looking like fool."

"There are no mistakes in pottery. Only 'happy accidents.'" She slipped on another bat.

"Wasn't that what Bob Ross, the PBS painter, said?"

"It applies to clay, too. It's all art." She hiked a shoulder and picked up the rest of the clay. She formed a grapefruit-sized ball. "Here, catch." She tossed the clay to him.

He caught it midair. "I'm still not so sure about this. I'm not actually known for my creative thinking."

She held a hand up to her chest. "I'm shocked."

Gabe made his way to the pottery wheel and got seated. Fiona positioned herself across from the wheel and walked him through each of the initial steps of centering the clay. He then began to shape the bowl just as he'd watched each of the kids do.

"Easy. You don't use strength. You use control." She leaned close and placed gentle hands over his. "Clay will respond, but you have to make the moves." She met his gaze and held it for a second.

"I understand." He returned his attention to the bowl and swallowed hard. Between her touch and her words, he found concentration impossible. He lifted his gaze from the bowl to see her face, but she was focused on the work.

"Always be aware of what you're doing." She unconsciously licked her lips. "One little change makes a big difference. Push too hard, too soon and it's over."

His hand slipped and the bowl became wonky. "Like that."

A sweet, bubbly laugh erupted from her lips. "You were so close."

He sighed. "Can you fix it?"

"Possibly, but do I want to?"

"Please."

"By the way, we don't fix. We refine." She nudged him out of the way, and began to reshape the clay. Under the power of her hands, she created a foot to the bottom of the bowl and then made a center with her thumb. The walls of the bowl grew upward, becoming thinner between the thumb and forefinger of her right hand. Her left, she said, provided counter pressure. When the bowl was nearly five inches in diameter, she lifted her foot from the pedal. The wheel came to a stop and she carefully flared the top like a ruffle.

"That's beautiful."

"Thank you." She stood and carefully removed the bat to the table. "I love working with clay. It reminds me that God is still shaping me. I pictured your bowl in my head before I went to work. I knew how I wanted it to turn out. I know He's the Creator and He knows what He wants me to be. He knows my purpose even when I'm not sure what it is."

"Fiona, I wish—"

"No, let's not talk about that today. It's been much too fun to delve into any of that." She wiped down the tablecloth and removed it. In silence, they cleaned up the remainder of the mess. She pointed to the bats holding the vessels. "We'll have to take these to my car."

"You didn't drive, remember?" He removed his apron, then motioned for her to spin around so he could untie hers.

"Oh, yeah, then I guess we'll put them in my office."

"We can take them to your friend's shop in my car." He folded the aprons and stuffed them on a shelf.

"From what I could tell, your car has never seen a dust mite let alone wet clay."

"We can use a trash bag or something to put under them, right?" Gabe headed toward the door. "I'll go find a cart to carry the bats on. I'd hate for my new bowl to get ruined. Wait until my mom sees what I made."

She was still shaking her head and grinning when he left the room.

He liked making her smile. He not only loved her laugh, he also loved watching how she interacted with others, especially children. Every day with Fiona was an adventure, and his life was sorely lacking in that area.

Tomorrow was their last day working together. He'd miss the kids, but more than that, he'd miss her. In their short time together, they'd become friends. He felt something for her that he might want to explore, but what about her? Did she share the same feelings? He'd sensed that her statements about pottery held double meanings. She'd said not to push too hard or too soon or things would be over, so, did he dare ask to see her outside of work? And given what he was going to have to recommend to the board, did he even want to go down this road?

CHAPTER 14

Fiona arrived early wearing one of her favorite Wacky Wednesday outfits—red bell-bottom pants with pom poms sewn on the hems, a pair of yellow suspenders, and a rainbow striped t-shirt. Instead of a hat, she'd chosen a bow that matched her shirt.

She used her extra time to groom Buttons. She brushed his coat and trimmed his nails. Every day, she tried to give Buttons ample time outside the Flophouse to roam, so when she was finished with his care, she let him hop around the room.

At exactly eight, she heard a knock on the door. She looked up to see Gabe enter, wearing a crisp, white tailored dress shirt.

"You are way underdressed for Wacky Wednesday." She walked around him in a slow circle, tapping her lip with her finger. "But I think I can come up with something."

He stood with his hands on his hips like Superman. "Fiona, I think I look fine."

Oh, he looked fine all right. "What you're wearing works for the office, but not for Wacky Wednesday." She opened a cabinet and rummaged through a plastic container. She returned with a giant elasticized blue bow tie, a red bandana, and a curly pink wig.

Gabe backed away from her. "Noooo way. I am not wearing that." He pointed to the wig.

"Oh, all right." She tossed it back into the container, then handed him the other two items. "Put the tie on and stick that bandana in your pocket." She demonstrated where on her own front. "Hang it down the front like a rodeo clown. I'll find you a hat instead of the wig."

When she returned from the cabinet, her lips curled into a wide smile. She popped a sparkly red cowboy hat on his head. "Now, that's more like it, partner."

He scowled. "I look like a clown."

"Exactly!" She picked up her purple bag.

He crossed his arms over his chest. "You do realize that people know me here."

"Not today. You're incognito."

"And you're delusional." He tugged at the bow tie. "And this is itchy."

She scooped up Buttons. "You'll live. Besides, if you hadn't blown me off on Monday, yesterday would have been your last day with me. Consider yourself lucky that you get one more day with yours truly."

He put his hand on door handle, but didn't open it. "What if I want more?"

"You want to shadow me longer?"

He turned and took the rabbit from her hands. "No, I want more time with you. Outside of the hospital. One date."

Her mouth felt as if she'd swallowed the pink wig. Her stomach twisted. How could he be interested in her? She had not seen this coming—or had she, a little. Hadn't she wondered what it would be like in his arms? But he wasn't thinking this through, and she was standing in front of him looking like a giant crayon box. "You can't be serious. Remember, you think I'm a clown and a fool."

"I was the fool. I didn't understand what you did and why you are so exceptional at doing it." He adjusted the bow on her head. "I just don't want today to be our last day together."

"But it won't be if you understand my program now. You've seen what I can do for the kids, so you won't suggest they cut Child Life, and we'll see each other all the time."

His shoulders slumped. "Fiona, I'm still going to have to recommend we eliminate the Child Life Program. I don't see another way."

Anger flared in her chest. Did he think he was some great consolation prize? "So, asking me out is your way of letting me down easy? No thanks."

"You know that that isn't what I'm saying." His voice was soft and calm. He held Buttons close and stroked his coat. "I'm standing here with a sparkly cowboy hat on my head and a rabbit in my arms ready to go with you anywhere, but I won't push you."

She saw raw honesty on his face and she fought for a reason to tell him no. Didn't he realize that she was broken? They had nothing in common. "But we're from different worlds. This is crazy."

"I'm asking for one day, Fiona. You take chances all the time. Take a chance on us."

She blinked and bit her lip. "I need time to think."

"Why? So you can talk yourself out of it?" He slipped the purple bag from her shoulder and handed her Buttons. "Remember, I have a whole day to convince you otherwise."

Fiona stood there staring as he walked back toward the door carrying her purple bag on his shoulder. Her heart spun like a top, making her breath come in short gasps. What if she had an anxiety attack now?

If she started anything with Gabe, how long would it take for him to realize how truly broken she was?

He jingled the bell on her scooter and raised his eyebrows

like Groucho Marx. "Say 'yes' and you can take the scooter."

Why should she fight him? He could be adorable in a businessman-turned-clown sort of way, and she felt like they had become friends. Besides, it wasn't like "yes" meant forever.

She smiled and brushed a crop of curls off her forehead. "Oh, all right. One date. Now, hand over the scooter and no one gets hurt."

Gabe stared at his computer screen but found it hard to concentrate on the spreadsheet's facts and figures. A week ago, he would have attacked his "to do" list with gusto, but today, his first back in his office, he kept thinking about the patients in pediatrics. Had Fiona gotten that one little boy to talk after she finally finished the monkey game? And what about Amazing Avery, the first kid he'd met? Were his blood counts holding? And he couldn't help but think about Alexis and the life she now faced as an amputee.

And what was the joke of the day?

He reached for the phone to call Fiona and ask but set the receiver back in its cradle with a click. Calling her would be unprofessional.

He took a swig of coffee and leaned back in his chair. How had one week with Fiona messed him up so badly? It had been easy to see if the budgets for each department were staying on course and address any problem areas. Patients didn't have faces. They were just another component in the equation to consider. After all, according to Case, cash was king.

The general public had no clue how complicated the hospital funding situation was. He wondered if Fiona had any idea.

Financing for hospital services came from a multitude of private insurers as well as Medicaid and Medicare programs, and of course, a percentage comes from the out-of-pocket costs paid by patients. What the average person would find even more difficult to comprehend was that the various insurance companies pay with an even wider assortment of methods with pre-arranged discounted charges and retrospective cost-based reimbursement.

He shook his head. It was enough to boggle the mind and he understood it. The whole billing process became a nightmare when one took into account how each department such as surgery, respiratory therapy, physical therapy, and occupational therapy billed separately for their time and services. How could they bill for the services of Fiona's Child Life Department? He didn't imagine a parent would want a bill for rabbit or magic time. Instead, the hospital had to consider it as overhead, like electricity or maintenance or social services, and that part of the budget could only stretch so far.

Monday, he would have to make a recommendation to the board. He dreaded the thought for so many reasons, not the least of which was letting Fiona down. But even if he made the recommendation, her department wouldn't necessarily have to close until the end of the fiscal year. That would give him even more time to find a possible alternative solution. God would have to lead him to that, however, because he'd already looked under all the rocks he knew of.

His desk phone buzzed and he lifted the receiver. Gerri informed him he had a call on line two from Miss McGrath.

"Fiona?" His heart rate picked up as his concern grew. Was something wrong with one of the kids?

"Hey, why did the cookie go to the hospital?"

Her cheerful voice set his mind at ease. "What did you say?"

"I thought you'd want to hear the joke of the day, so why did the cookie go to the hospital?"

He smiled to himself. "I don't know. Why?"

"Because he felt crumby." She laughed softly even though he guessed she'd told the joke at least a dozen times today.

"Speaking of lunch, I'm headed that way soon. Want to join me?"

"I can't. I have to give a tour of the hospital to some pediatric patients who will be having their tonsils out in the near future. I scheduled it over the lunch hour because most of the parents can come then and not miss work. I'd tell you to leave a little for me in the cafeteria, but I've seen how much you eat and I won't have time anyway."

He said he'd catch up with her later. Although he was disappointed, he at least had Saturday to look forward to. The weatherman predicted to have a high of seventy-two degrees. From sunrise to sunset, he was going to make the most of the day, so he hoped Fiona wasn't a woman who liked to sleep in.

Giving hospital tours was one of Fiona's favorite jobs. She liked how it prepared children for what was to come and helped alleviate their fears. She'd explained, with the help of her doll, how they might get an IV, a little straw for medicine, in their arm, and how they would wear a pulse oximeter, a bandage with a light. The blood pressure cuff, she'd told them, was like a hug for their arm. She'd shown them the little red wagon in which they'd ride to surgery and the pajamas they'd put on. She let them each smell the anesthesia mask and explained that the kids could pick a scent—orange, grape, cherry, strawberry, or bubblegum. In the operating room, she was careful to point out that it would be cold, there'd be lots of machines, and everyone would be wearing masks and hairnets.

The children loved reenacting what she'd told them at the end when she gave them time for some medical play. Before the families left, she made sure the parents knew to show the kids a video link that would reinforce what they'd talked about today. She also gave the parents a brochure designed specifically for them and reminded them to call her if they had questions or concerns.

She mentally checked the tour off her list of tasks for the day and considered what was left to complete as she made her way back to her office. She had a nine-year-old boy who'd had surgery on his arm early this morning. As soon as he got back to the pediatric unit, she wanted to touch base with the parents. She had some basic pain management techniques to share with them.

She swung by the snack bar and grabbed an apple and a bag of chips. Not the healthiest of lunches, but it was better than nothing. She bit into the juicy apple and hit the elevator button. It dinged right away. Since she was missing lunch, she'd brew a cup of tea when she got back to her office. It was one of the ways she could sneak in a few moments for herself in a day focused on the needs of others.

After entering her office, she deposited her bag and medical play doll on the table and tossed the unopened bag of chips on her desk. She ran a cup of water through her coffee maker, added a heaping tablespoon of chai tea mix, and stirred. She sat down in her office chair and inhaled the cinnamon scent of the spiced tea. She took a sip. Delicious. She willed her body to relax and leaned into the ergonomic support of the chair. If she stayed there too long, she'd fall asleep.

Her moment of relaxation evaporated at the sound of a hard knock on the door. She called for the person to come in, but when she did, Fiona nearly dropped her tea.

She stared at her sister. Her real sister. "Shannon, what are you doing here?"

CHAPTER 15

Stepping off the elevator, Gabe resituated the salad and the cookies in his hands. If Fiona couldn't go to lunch, lunch could come to her. He made his way directly to Fiona's office, but stopped outside the door when he heard raised female voices inside. He recognized Fiona's, but not the other one. Was it a patient's mother? A staff member? Whoever the other woman was, she was clearly upset.

"You don't really care at all!"

He didn't like the woman's accusation, but should he interrupt?

"Shannon, please calm down." He'd heard Fiona use that same tone with unruly children. "You know the boundaries I've set. I will not give you any more money—whether it's to pay a bill, buy you food, or put gas in your car."

"But I'm starving!" The woman screeched. "I oughta teach you a lesson once and for all, you little—"

That was it. Gabe thrust open the door. Both Fiona and the woman she'd called Shannon turned startled faces toward him.

"Did someone say that they were starving?" He held up the salad and glanced at Fiona. She nodded and he handed it to the unfamiliar woman.

"Gabe, this is my sister, Shannon."

He gave the woman a quick perusal. Although he recalled that Fiona only had a younger sister, this woman looked years older than Fiona. Her clothes reeked of body odor and something like lighter fluid. She was bone thin, her eyes were bloodshot, and she made spastic movements with her hands. "Your younger sister, right?"

"The very one." Fiona stood, ramrod stiff, and walked to the door. "And she was just leaving."

"You're heartless." She glared at Fiona. At the door, she whirled toward her. "The only person you care about is yourself."

Tears glistened in Fiona's eyes. "Shannon, you know I care about you. I love you and I pray for you. I want you to be well and safe, but like I told you, if you want to talk to me—to really talk to me—or if you're willing to get treatment, let Ambrose know where I can get in touch with you. I'll be there for you."

"I'm homeless, but you wouldn't know about that. You sit in your fancy place and don't worry about a soul except for yourself. Why can't I know the address?"

Gabe clenched his jaw as the hair on his neck prickled. The last thing he wanted was for Shannon and her friends to know where Fiona lived. Should he simply call security and have her escorted out of the hospital?

Fiona drew in a long breath. Then, she cleared her throat, squared her shoulders, and spoke in a calm, firm voice. "You know one of my boundaries is no more insults or ridicule. I have a right to expect decent and respectful behavior—even from you. You also know why you can't have my address."

Shannon curled her lip and sneered, "Your therapist told you to say that, didn't she?"

Fiona opened the door. "Goodbye, Shannon."

With her hand still on the door, Fiona stood in the hall until Shannon was on the elevator. Then, she walked back inside, closed the door, and turned to Gabe. "You'd better go, too. I'm about to lose it."

"I'm not going anywhere."

Her legs seemed unable to hold her any longer. She slid her back down the length of the wall and dropped her head into her hands. Sobs wracked her body.

What was he supposed to do now? Sure, he'd seen his mom and sisters cry, but this was more than simple tears. This was anguish and heartbreak, and he had no idea what to do. He'd never felt so helpless. *Please God, help me help Fiona.*

He spotted a box of tissues on her desk and picked them up. He then lowered himself down to the floor. Her body shook beside him. He slipped his arm around her shoulders and pulled her close. The faint floral scent of her shampoo whispered to him. She gave in to his embrace, and he felt a surge of protectiveness. He'd do anything to keep her from hurting like this again.

After a few minutes, her sobs quieted and she reached for the tissue box he'd set in front of her. She wiped her face and noisily blew her nose.

She pulled away from him. "I'm sorry."

"What are you sorry for? You didn't do anything. She barged into your office, or so I'm guessing, and asked for money or something, right?"

Fiona nodded and swiped fresh tears.

"Shannon made those choices. Not you." His chest heaved with frustration at Shannon. "Has she stolen from you in the past?"

"She has. That's why she can't know where I live."

He pushed to his feet and reached out his hand to Fiona. She took it and allowed him to help her to feet. "How long has she been an addict?"

"Four years." She released his hand and walked to the window. "When I turned eighteen, I went to college. When she turned eighteen, she went to shack up with her pusher boyfriend. I get so angry with her and at the same time I love her. I know it's a disease. I work in the health profession and should be able to handle myself better, but she says things to push my buttons. She wants to make me angry."

"I thought you handled her as well as anybody could. I was proud of you. You didn't let her push you around, and yet, you made sure she knew you cared."

She turned to him, fresh tears making her eyes glisten. "I don't want her to die. And every time she leaves, I spend a week on 'what ifs.' What if I didn't say the right words? What if I'd helped her just this once? What if she really is starving? What if I did give her my address so she could find me if she needed me? What if that was the last time I ever see her?"

"Fiona, I'm sure that it's terrifying, and nothing I can say will take that away. But remember God loves her and He's pursuing her. You can never do more than He can."

"You're a pretty smart guy." She gave him a wry smile. "Bet you wish you would've left when you had the chance."

"No. Never."

Why did she always expect him to leave her? Had everyone bailed on her?

Well, he wasn't like that. Somehow, he had to get her to understand he had no intention of going anywhere.

Sand therapy would most likely not be on the table once her therapist, Laura Batista, heard about Fiona's week. If she did get to use the sand tray, she wondered how she could make a sink hole in the center, swallowing everything and everyone in its wake. That would be the best representation of this week, and she'd love to see Laura interpret that.

When Laura called her into the consultation room, Fiona curled up in her favorite comfy chair and grabbed a faux fur pillow to hold against her chest. She sighed.

Laura hiked up her purple glasses and peered at her. "Long week?"

"The longest." She drew in a deep breath. "Love the glasses with the silver outfit, by the way."

Laura thanked her. "When last we talked, you were deciding if you'd go to a family picnic. What did you decide?"

Fiona explained the whole situation and how supportive she'd found Gabe's mother to be. She also admitted how they'd parted on bad terms at the end because he'd thought she would abandon her kids.

Laura jotted notes on a tablet. "Did you resolve your issues?"

Fiona smiled. "You could say that."

The therapist's eyes narrowed. "I sense there's more to this story."

Fiona decided it was worthless to hide anything from Laura. She spilled everything from the cut on her finger, to telling Gabe about her messed-up family, to agreeing to see him for a date on Saturday night.

Laura looked up from her notepad. "How did you feel about him knowing your family history?"

"I was ashamed, embarrassed, mortified. His family is so normal and mine is so messed up. The entire night was overwhelming. It was the same night I had a teenage patient who had to have her leg amputated. The whole time is sort of a blur."

"And how did your friend react to the story of your past?"

"He was sympathetic. He gave me the pity treatment, but I set him right. He didn't leave me."

Laura smiled. "You expected him to?"

"I think I did." Fiona paused. "He was there yesterday when Shannon showed up, too."

"Your sister came to the hospital? How did that go?"

Laura listened as Fiona shared the details and her fears, but occasionally posed clarifying questions. "It sounds like you remembered the boundaries we've talked about and still made sure your sister knew you had her best interests at heart."

"I never feel like I'm saying or doing the right stuff."

"Fiona, remember, you have to be relentless because she's an addict. It's better that she becomes uncomfortable. She has to become tired enough of the life she's currently living before she will work on getting a new one. It's like someone who makes a decision to lose weight. They have to become tired of carrying the extra pounds before they're willing to do the work to get it off."

"But how can I help her and push her away at the same time? She only wanted fifty dollars."

Laura paused for a second. "And how would you feel if she used that fifty dollars to buy the drugs that led to an overdose that killed her?"

Fiona considered the question, her shoulders drooping. "I couldn't live with myself."

Laura leaned forward and placed a hand on Fiona's arm. "You did the right thing for yourself and for Shannon." She sat back. "Did anything else happen in regard to your sister?"

Fiona hugged the pillow more tightly. "My brother, Ambrose, came to my place to warn me Shannon was in town. After he left, I had an anxiety attack. The first in months."

"And how did you handle it?"

"I went through the steps you've taught me. I think it was the shortest one I've had." Fiona shared exactly what she had done. "And I remembered that an anxiety attack is just my body preparing to fight."

"Well done." Laura smiled broadly. "So tell me more about this Gabe. Isn't he the man who was trying to shut down your program? Were you able to convince him of your program's value?"

"Yes, but—" Fiona's mind raced. How was she going to explain this in a way that made any sense? "He understands and respects the work I do, but he still can't find a way to fit it into the hospital budget."

"I see. But you said he was with you today when your sister came?"

"He brought me lunch." Her lips curled at the thought. "But he gave it to Shannon because she said she was starving. He stayed until after she left and.... Well, we're spending Saturday together."

"You started to say something else happened after Shannon left. What was it?"

"I cried. A lot."

"What did he do then?"

"Held me."

"And he didn't leave you." Laura leaned back in her chair.

"You've had quite a week, Fiona. How do you feel you've handled it all?"

"So-so, I guess. Too much crying, not enough praying?"

"But you did pray, didn't you?"

"I did. It seems like I was praying at every turn. I still don't feel like I did enough. I let my kids down, and I let myself down. I don't want give up on the Child Life Program."

"Follow me." Laura stood and led Fiona to an oval wall mirror with a bronze frame. She directed Fiona to stand before it and moved to stand behind her. "What do you see?"

"A lot of orange hair."

"And?"

"Pale skin and freckles."

"You know what I see?" She placed her hands on Fiona's shoulders. "I see a woman who has grown immensely in the last year. I see a strong woman who has faced her demons with courage and has opened her heart to others. I see a woman who has let God begin to heal her hurts." She paused as if she were waiting for her words to sink in. "But I also see a woman who has one more mountain to climb. It will be the hardest one. It's the one where you learn to believe in your value as much as the rest of us already do. It's the one where you learn to believe that when God said He will meet all your needs, that He will do it. His promises aren't for everyone else, Fiona. They're for you."

Hot tears trailed down Fiona's cheeks. *His promises are for me.* She wanted to believe them. In her head, she knew everything Laura had said was true, but her heart still doubted.

Always, always, always doubted.

CHAPTER 16

Fiona's Friday afternoon therapy sessions wore her out, and today had been no exception. When she got to her apartment, she kicked off her shoes and changed into sweats and a t-shirt. She made a quick call to Mom Cat to touch base and shared some of what her therapist had said. Of course, she didn't share every detail. Still, Mom Cat seemed to have a second sense about such things.

"So what are your plans for the weekend?" Mom Cat asked.

Fiona admitted she was spending the day with Gabe, and yes, he was the same man who had been shadowing her last week.

"He must have been won over by your sarcastic charm." Mom Cat laughed, then grew serious. "Fiona, if you think there could be something, don't push him away. You're ready for love."

Ready for love? Was anybody ever ready for love? And especially her—the woman soon-to-be without a job, with an addicted sister, a dad in prison, and a dead mother?

Mom Cat didn't push her about the subject. Instead, she told her to have fun and that she'd see her Sunday. Before she hung up, she told Fiona that the girls, Solana and Talia, were wondering if Fiona could take them dress shopping for their Winter Formal. "Apparently," Mom Cat said, "they think I'm too old to make a fashionable selection."

"Talia wants me to come?"

"Not exactly, but Talia doesn't want anyone around, ever. I'm hoping you can still get through to her."

Fiona agreed to set Sunday afternoon aside for them, praying that somehow she could make a connection with Talia.

After Fiona said goodbye, she made an omelet and took a long, hot bath. A quick check of tomorrow's weather told her the day would be nice, but the evening might get cool. She had the perfect outfit.

She checked her phone one more time for a text from Gabe about when he was coming to pick her up. If she didn't hear from him tonight, she was certain she would in the morning. Hopefully, he wouldn't call until well after ten. It had been an exhausting week and a girl needed her beauty sleep. After double checking the locks on the door, she curled up with a book in bed until sleep claimed her.

She startled awake at the sound of her phone's ringtone and grabbed the device. It was Gabe. She answered with a groggy "hello."

"Good morning. If you'll buzz me in, we can get an early start to the day."

She looked at the time. "It's not even eight o'clock. Do you have a death wish?"

"Fiona, are you going to buzz me in or make me stand here all day?"

He was way too cheery for pre-coffee time.

"I stopped for macchiatos," he crooned.

She sat bolt upright as his words seeped through her foggy brain. He intended to come in now! "Gabe, I'm not even dressed. I mean I have clothes on, but not the ones—"

"Relax. I'll wait while you get ready. I should have called you last night and shared my plans. I figured that if I only get one day, I want all of it."

She liked the warmth in his voice, but hated the thought of

facing him with bedhead.

After tossing back her covers, she stuffed her feet into slippers, wiggled into a bra, and then glanced at her reflection in the mirror. An explosion of curls covered her head. She twisted her hair into a topknot and secured it with a scrunchy. It would have to do.

She buzzed him in and, a minute later, he was at her door. When she opened it, he held out a macchiato like a peace offering. "It's called a cocoa cloud. I knew you liked chocolate." He eyed her t-shirt and chuckled. "Good for you."

Huh? Fiona glanced down to see what she was wearing. Her shirt read "I love Jesus and I have a therapist." Perfect. Wasn't that a lovely way to start a date?

Her cheeks heated. "I think I'll go get dressed. Give me at least forty-five minutes, okay?" She passed him the remote for the television. "I have no idea what is on at eight on a Saturday morning, but maybe you can find cartoons or something."

She took a final glance at his clothing to decide how casual to dress. He looked good in a pair of well-fitting jeans, an untucked pale gray shirt, and a pair of loafers. Good. Their day appeared to not require formal attire. If it had, she would have needed more than forty-five minutes.

She took every minute of her allotted time to get ready, but when she emerged from her bedroom, she felt confident in a white, flowy boho dress with a crocheted bodice, and comfy boots. She carried a cropped denim jacket in case it got cool. She completed the ensemble with a wide-brimmed felt hat, which was always a good accessory beneath the Florida sun any time of the year.

Gabe stood and smiled when she came out. "That was certainly worth the wait. You look great."

"Thank you." She finished her macchiato and tossed the empty cup in the trash. "And thank you for that, too. Will this outfit work for what you have planned? Cause if you're planning on making me ride a bicycle for twenty-five miles, I'd better change and pack some oxygen."

"What you're wearing is fine." He chuckled and stepped to the door. "Ready?"

Before following him out, she grabbed her purse and phone and checked the locks. He held the car door for her, and her heart fluttered. She ordered it to be still. There was something undeniable in the air, and it was stronger than his heady cologne.

Since they hadn't seen each other yesterday, they had a lot to catch up on while they drove to Tarpon Springs.

"I'm sure you've been here hundreds of times, but I was hoping it would be fun to explore together." He turned onto Tarpon Avenue.

"Actually, I've never been to the touristy part of Tarpon. I think my Tarpon Springs experience has been relegated to high school football games."

"A virgin then." He suddenly realized what he'd said and his cheeks colored to a bright pink. "I'm sorry, I didn't—"

"It's okay. I knew what you meant."

About twenty minutes later, he pulled up to a large Victorian style mint green house with white and purple trim. The sign in front read "The 1910 Inn: Historic Bed and Breakfast." She cocked her head to the side and bit her lip. What were they doing at a bed and breakfast? Had she given him the wrong idea?

"I talked to Annie, the innkeeper, and asked if she could fit us in for breakfast. She's setting us up on the veranda." He parked the car. "I'm told her food is amazing."

They approached the rounded veranda and climbed the stairs. Inside, Fiona sucked in her breath at the sight of an ornately carved staircase. The house had been beautifully preserved or restored. Fiona wondered what the rooms looked like upstairs. Within a minute, they were greeted by Annie.

"You must be Gabe and Fiona." She shook their hands. "Let's get you to your table."

They followed her out the veranda to a round glass-topped wrought iron table. She turned to Fiona. "I set that blanket on the chair in case you get chilly out here. I'll be out with your breakfasts in a few minutes."

A young woman soon appeared and set glasses of orange juice and water in front of each of them.

Fiona snagged the blanket and covered her legs. The morning temps were still low and the breeze made gooseflesh appear on her arms. Gabe, however, looked perfectly comfortable.

Annie returned with delicious piles of butter pecan French toast. She also set down bowls of Greek yoghurt with fresh raspberries and honey and explained that it was a traditional Greek breakfast.

Gabe held out his hand, palm up, towards Fi. She put her chilled hand in his warm one as he led a prayer for them, asking God to bless their day together.

"Listen to all the birds." Fiona paused after her first bite of French toast had melted on her tongue. "Sometimes I forget how blessed we are to live here. Everywhere you look, you can see nature."

He leaned back in his chair and listened. "I wish I'd been a better Boy Scout. If I had been, maybe I could recognize some of their songs."

"So you were a Boy Scout." She poured honey over her yoghurt and sprinkled it with berries. "It figures."

"I'm guessing from that comment that you were not a Girl Scout."

"No, but I was in 4-H. I had rabbits. Grand Champion Showman my senior year."

"Why does that not surprise me?" He grinned. "How's the yoghurt with the honey?"

"Delicious. I like the contrast between the tang of the yoghurt and the sweetness of the honey." She dabbed at her lips. "So are you going to tell me about your plans for the rest of the day?"

"No, I think I'll just make you trust me." Their gazes locked and held.

"Trusting people isn't exactly my strong suit."

"I know."

Fiona reached for her water. That man's eyes were lethal.

Excitement coursed through Gabe as he took Fiona's hand and walked from the inn toward Craig Park and the Spring Bayou. She hadn't pulled away, and that was a start.

Stately homes lined the street side of the bayou, but a park, set on a sort of peninsula, allowed them to get a better look at the water. They followed the sidewalk around to a statue of Ama of Tarpon Springs, a six-foot-tall bronze mermaid. The site, he'd been told, was one of the best places to spot a manatee.

Fiona studied the statue. "I guess she has legs because she's on land right now, but she's carrying her scales and tails for when she goes back to the water."

"Your guess is as good as mine. Let's go to the edge of the wall and see what we can find in the water. Maybe we'll see a mermaid." He grinned and tugged her toward the sparkling waters. He was glad he'd worn his sunglasses and put sunscreen on his smooth pate. The sun was bright.

"Look!" Despite the brim on her hat, Fiona shielded her eyes with her hand and pointed toward the water. "Is that a manatee?"

"It sure is." They walked toward the water's edge. "The bayou is fed by a warm spring. The sea cows like it here."

"I've only seen them in pictures." She leaned so far over the edge that Gabe grabbed hold of her waist to keep her from falling. A mother manatee and a calf swam near in the clear water. "They're amazing!"

He motioned farther out. "There's more over there." One of them flipped onto its back and floated by. "They like to graze just like cows."

"I'm dumbstruck. I didn't know there were manatees here." She stepped back from the edge and Gabe released his hold. "The only thing I've heard about this area is the cross dive the Greek Orthodox church does on Epiphany."

"It's quite an event. I went a few years ago. Have you ever been?"

"No, remember?"

Oh, yeah, she was a Tarpon Springs virgin. He'd not make that mistake again. He smiled down at her. "Thousands of people come here to the Spring Bayou to watch young Orthodox Greeks dive into the water to retrieve a white cross. It's quite a festival."

"How many men dive?"

He shrugged. "I think there were about fifty or so. They're all teens, actually. The year I went, a seventeen-year-old diver found it. Tradition is that he would have a whole year of blessings for being the one to retrieve it."

"I'd sure like a whole year of blessings, but I suppose I already have that—every day of every year."

He looked down at her, but he couldn't see her eyes beneath the brim of the hat.

"Gabe, there's a dolphin!" She grabbed his arm, bouncing on her toes. "Do you see it?"

"I do."

The dolphin leapt in the water and she squealed with delight. "Can we stay here all day?"

He shrugged. "Until you get bored or I get hungry again—whichever comes first."

She laughed and removed her hat. She tipped her face up to his. "Thank you. I do feel blessed."

He grinned and squeezed her hand. "I'll work on that whole year part later."

After a lunch of Greek gyros, Fiona followed Gabe through the historic Sponge Dock area of Tarpon Springs along the Anclote River. He led her to a boat proudly displaying the name *St. Nicholas VII* across its bow. When the boat was ready to board, he presented his tickets and helped her climb up into the vessel.

Bench style seating rimmed the boat's interior, and they sat down near the front. The captain climbed aboard as did another older gentleman and a man in an old-fashioned diving suit. They untied the moorings and the captain started the engine before heading for open water.

Gabe had obviously heard the captain's spiel before, but this was a first for her. She listened closely as the captain explained the history of sponging in Tarpon Springs. She was shocked to find out that it began in the late 1800s and by the turn of the century, over five hundred divers were collecting sponges. At the height of the sponge industry, they were harvesting over three million dollars' worth of sponges.

She shook her head. Sponges? What in the world for?

Gabe slipped his arm around her and she leaned against him. It felt right, not forced or awkward, and she liked the warmth. The cool breeze caused by their travel had chilled her.

The captain drew the boat to a stop, and the two men began to help the diver, dressed in historic garb, put on the rest of his gear. He laced up weighted boots, and the men secured a collar around his neck with wingnuts and bolts. When they added the helmet, they were able to lock it into the collar. The diver then moved to the aft of the ship and sat on the edge. Once his suit was inflated, he dove in with a sponge hook in his hand. A long hose connected him to the oxygen on the ship.

Foamy bubbles rose from where he swam. A few minutes later, he returned with a fresh, dark sponge. According to their hosts, sponges like this would be cleaned, trimmed and graded in huge warehouses. At the Sponge Exchange, the captain said, men would bid on piles of sponges.

Gabe leaned close. "Are you enjoying yourself?"

"I am. This is fascinating." She looked at the faces of the children passengers. "They are too."

"Did you know that they used sponges in surgery for a long time? They are naturally antimicrobial. They've been used for everything from water filters to cleaning to contraceptives."

"Oh." Heat flared in her cheeks. "And here I just wanted one for my bath."

After the *St. Nicholas* was secured at the dock, Gabe suggested they do a little shopping. They perused shops, smelling goat milk and olive oil soaps, listening to wind chimes, and examining all kinds of sponges: cosmetic sponges, bath sponges, vase sponges, and giant decorative sponges. Fiona purchased a goat milk soap and sponge set in one shop.

Gabe stopped in front of the Tarpon Springs Olive Oil Company. "Let's try this one."

"Are you sure? I'm not much of a cook."

"But I am." He grinned and opened the door.

Small, silver vats with spigots lined the walls. The clerk explained that each of these vats were called "fustis" and was marked with its contents. They tasted tiny cups of fig, lavender, and cinnamon pear flavored balsamic vinegar along with many others.

"These would certainly turn a traditional boring salad into real treat," she admitted.

They laughed at some of the items offered like espresso and dark chocolate balsamic vinegar, but the clerk insisted both were wonderful with the right combinations.

"I agree. The real trick is in the pairing." Gabe put a dab of blood orange olive oil in a cup and added a splash of the dark chocolate balsamic vinegar. He passed her his creation. "Here, try this."

The tangy, sweet mixture exploded on her tongue. "Wow. That's delicious. How'd you know this would be so good together?"

He cupped her cheek and used the pad of his thumb to wipe a bit of the mixture from her lips. His gaze locked on hers. "I've got a good sense about what will fit together. Some of the best pairings in life have very little in common." He licked his thumb.

She felt a slightly lightheaded. Maybe it was the vinegar. Did Gabe really mean that in the way he seemed to imply?

She needed to be careful. Even he realized they had little in common, and on a day like today, it was easy to forget how substantial those differences were. If she cared about this man, and she believed she did, she needed to protect him from her and her crazy life.

"Don't push him away." Mom Cat's words came back to her.

But what if she was pushing him away for his own good?

CHAPTER 17

More people began to fill the sidewalks as evening approached. Gabe suggested they put their purchases in the car before they continued their adventure. Fiona also took the opportunity to leave her hat and retrieve her jacket to be ready for cooler evening temperatures.

When they returned to Dodecanese Street, Fiona grabbed Gabe's arm. "What are they setting up all those tables for?"

"It's 'A Night in the Islands' celebration. Greek music, food, and dance under the stars on the docks, right by the water just like in Greece." As if he'd summoned it by the mere mention, a group of young men began playing Greek music on their bouzoukis. The sound of the bulbous guitar-like instrument was lilting and melodic. The rhythm and tempo begged one to dance.

Fiona turned toward the sound, so Gabe placed his hand on her back and encouraged her to walk in that direction. The fingers of the players flew over their stringed instruments, creating the intricate music.

Fiona clasped her hands together in front of her and bounced to the music.

Gabe turned when he heard a woman call out from the street that she was going to teach the Greek dance called the *Kalamotiano*. A circle of patrons formed around her.

He leaned close to Fiona's ear. "When in Rome...or in our case Tarpon Springs—"

He didn't have to finish since Fiona nodded enthusiastically.

With Fiona's hand clasped in his, he led them toward the circle where they joined hands with strangers. They followed the teacher's lead, placing one foot forward, the next behind, and the third to the right. The next steps were a blur to Gabe of stepping forward, backward, shuffling, and kicking, but Fiona seemed to pick them up easily. Gabe's heart swelled every time Fiona giggled or flashed him a wide grin.

He stumbled and fell against Fiona. His cheeks heated, but she laughed and made a display of showing him the steps, which she'd already mastered. After their lesson concluded, he suggested they head down the block toward Hellas, the restaurant at which he'd made reservations.

They were shown to their outdoor table, covered in a bright blue cloth. Since most of the tables were set for four to six or more people, they were told it was a night to make new friends. Disappointment nudged him inside. Perhaps he should have made reservations for a private table inside one of the restaurants.

He spread his napkin in his lap. "I hope you don't mind eating with strangers."

Fiona bobbed her head to the music. "Mom Cat says I've never actually met a stranger."

"Mom Cat?"

She covered her lips with her fingertips, then let her hand fall back to her side. "She's my foster mom."

"Is she a crazy cat lady or something?"

"No." Fiona giggled and resumed her head bobbing. "Her name is Catherine, but it felt weird when I came to her house to call someone else mom, so Mom Cat was my way of compromising, I guess."

"Smart even then. So that's where you went to live after what happened with your mom?"

"Eventually."

He draped his arm around the back of her chair, and nodded toward a couple being led to their table. "It appears we're about to meet our new neighbors."

It turned out to be an older couple visiting Tarpon Springs on vacation from Nebraska. This was their first Greek experience and the wife was giddy with excitement. She prodded Fiona and Gabe for suggestions. He told them everything was delicious, but they had to get an order of *Saganaki*.

Gabe asked Fiona what she wanted from the menu, and then added several extra selections when the waiter came to take their order. "I want you to be able to try a little of everything," he whispered in her ear.

"But octopus?"

"I won't make you eat it. I promise, but it's one of my favorites."

Once the sun had set, the string lights were turned on, creating a festive atmosphere. Between the music, the lights, and the outdoor seating, it was easy to imagine they were indeed in Greece.

Fiona's eyes grew wide as the Greek flaming cheese, *saganaki*, was served to the table next to them. The diners yelled, "Opa!" A few minutes later, their own orders of *saganaki* arrived. Their server poured brandy over the cheese and set it afire.

"Opa!" They yelled in unison.

Once the Greek brandy had burnt off, Gabe demonstrated how to dig in to the kasseri cheese with one's fork. The *saganaki* was brown and crusty on the outside and gooey inside. Strings of hot cheese led from his fork to the pan. He lifted the fork to Fiona's lips, and she accepted the offering. "Wow, that's my new favorite thing."

When the rest of their food arrived, Gabe suggested the four of them share the bounty as the older couple hadn't ordered a great variety. Spanakopita, a blend of spinach and cheese in a flaky filo dough, turned out to be at the top of Fiona's list, while the woman seated with them liked the *keftedes* or Greek style meatballs.

"Ew." Fiona's nose scrunched up when the waiter set a plate of grilled octopus in front of Gabe. "It's so little and leggy. Are you really going to eat that?"

"Absolutely. Want a bite?" He dangled a tentacle in front of her.

"No, thank you. I've read way too many kids books about octopi to even think about it." She snagged a *dolmade* and put it on her plate. "What's the meat wrapped in? Cabbage?"

"It's a grape vine leaf. The little rolls are topped with an egg lemon sauce."

"You really do cook, don't you?"

He nodded and swallowed. "Next week, I'll cook for you."

It was out before he realized what he was saying. Fiona seemed to take a sudden interest in her *dolmade*. Was she thinking about next week or wondering how to gracefully get out of it?

Why had he opened his big mouth? She'd warned him not to push, but he was a man who was used to going after what he wanted and getting it. Their day had been fantastic and one date was not going to be enough.

"Honey," the lady across from Fiona said, "if you've found a man who likes to cook, take it from me, you'd better hang on to him. He's a rare breed."

Fiona patted Gabe's arm. "As much as this guy eats, he'd better cook because a woman would kill herself trying to keep him full."

He speared a *dolmade* to add credence to her claim.

A Greek band with a talented baritone began to perform. As diners at the tables finished their food, several of Tarpon's Greek men and women persuaded the diners to come into the streets and dance with them. A woman took Gabe's hand and he, in turn, grabbed Fiona's. There was no way he was doing this alone.

This impromptu line dancing was not as formal as what they'd learned earlier, but he was glad he'd mastered a few steps, especially when others joined their line. All of them kept their joined hands held high, and Fiona fell in step with the woman as if she'd been doing the *Kalamatiano* all her life. The slow, quick, quick count was easy to follow, and he found himself watching her more than his own steps.

Fiona gave him a saucy, playful smile. She had finally allowed herself to let go, and was truly enjoying herself. Her joy was contagious. One song led to another, and they continued with the dancing. When the set ended, he caught Fiona up in his arms and swung her around, before setting her back on her feet.

She squealed and held onto his arms to steady herself. "Oh Gabe, that was wonderful!"

He wanted to kiss her, right then and there, but he stopped himself. Too much, too soon. With her guard finally down, he didn't want to do anything to make her bolt.

"Gabe, I think I've had enough noise for now," Fiona yelled over the din. "Do you mind if we find somewhere a little quieter?"

Once Gabe had paid the bill and they'd told their tablemates good-bye, he led her into the bakery side of Hellas. Pastries filled the glass display cases. Fiona had never seen so many selections.

Her stomach cinched at the site and she moaned. "Gabe, I can't eat another bite."

"These are for later. The day isn't complete without baklava." He grinned. "I suppose you'd like yours dipped in chocolate."

"If—and I do mean if—I ever get hungry again, the answer is yes, I'd like mine dipped in chocolate."

He placed an order while she perused the cookie assortment.

He glanced at her and grinned. "And add six each of the *ergolavos* with chocolate filling, the chocolate *kouluria*, and the *kourabiedes*."

"Wedding cookies, eh?" The clerk looked from him to Fiona and winked.

Fiona cheeks warmed, but she pretended not to see the display. She looked up when he approached and asked what was in the bag. "Gabe, what are you going to do with all of those?"

"Eat them, I hope—and not alone." He paid the cashier. "Consider them snacks for the week to remind us of tonight."

She giggled and slipped her hand into the crook of his arm. "In your hands, those snacks might last an hour."

They walked down the sidewalk for several blocks, away from the festivities and noise. When they neared the marina, Fiona paused in front of the bronze statue of a historic sponge diver.

"An entire area built around sponges. Who would have guessed?" She tipped her face toward him. "It's funny. I do feel like I've been to Greece today in a way. In a half-mile circle, this place is a world all its own. Thank you for bringing me."

The muted sounds of the Greek band drifted toward them. Instead of the fast music they'd performed earlier, they now played a slower, sweeter, more romantic tune.

"I may not be able to do the *Kalamatiano*, but even I can dance to this." Gabe held his palm out to her. "May I have this dance?"

She stared at his hand, her breath growing shallow. Dancing with him now, alone, would be far different than laughing in the streets. It would mean crossing the barrier she'd erected around herself—the I-can-be-fun-and-flirty-but-not-yours-forever wall. She could see it in his eyes. If she said yes, it would mean letting him into her life and her heart.

You're ready for love.

Mom Cat's words echoed in her mind. But was she ready? Unless she opened herself up to God's blessings, she'd never know them, but it was so hard to let go. *Please God, help me say yes this time.*

She placed her trembling hand in his. He lifted it to his lips and brushed her fingertips with a kiss. Then he drew her close, and she let the sweetness of the music, the magic of the day, and the warmth of his arms carry her away.

Maybe—just maybe—she was ready.

CHAPTER 18

"I like the color of that one on you." Fiona motioned for Talia, her new foster sister, to turn around in a circle. "The ice blue color is gorgeous."

Talia clawed at her neck. "But this part is so high it's choking me. I can't breathe."

Fiona laughed. At least Talia was being honest, and she'd take any communication she could get from the teenager. After church services, she'd taken the girls with her, but Talia had refused to do much communicating all the way through lunch and during the car ride to the boutique.

Fiona recalled her own dress shopping trips with Mom Cat. While there was a second-hand charity shop available to foster kids, Mom Cat didn't take her girls there. She wanted her girls to experience what all the other girls in the school did, which included shopping in a real shop from the rack. Fiona's first dress shopping trip, however, had been a killer. She'd probably been as morose as Talia.

The clerk eyed Talia's image in the mirror. "A halter neckline can feel a bit tight, but it really shows off the keyhole in the back. It's very fashionable, and of course it hurts. Beauty is pain."

Talia glared at the woman, and she slinked back to her place behind the front desk.

Fiona pressed her lips together, then sighed. "Well, I do love the beadwork, and it fits the school's dress code for formals at dances."

Talia crossed her arms over her chest. "That dress code is ridiculous. Do they think we're still living in the Middle Ages?"

Solana, who'd been perusing the racks, hurried over to join the fray. "Nothing more than four inches above your knee? You can't even find a short formal that is long enough if you happen to be tall like me."

"I understand it can be hard, but there are a lot of dress choices out there, and there's always the internet. We'll keep looking until we find one." Fiona thumbed through the dresses in front of her. She withdrew a hanger. "What about this one, Solana? It has a high-low hemline? And I love this coral color."

"Too bridesmaid-ish." Solana pulled out a different dress. "But what do you think about this one. It's that same color, but more my style. What do you call this hemline?"

"Handkerchief, and the V-neck isn't too low. Go try it on." Fiona turned to Talia. "You really aren't sold on that one, are you?"

"What was your first clue? I give up. These are all lame." She flopped down into a chair by the dressing room.

"I can't let you give up that easy." Fiona studied the young lady. She was a hard one to read. Just when Fiona felt like she was making progress building rapport with Talia, the girl put up another wall. And if anyone recognized walls, it was Fiona. She'd simply have to keep trying to break through both her own and Talia's. The teen may not realize it, but she needed her new family.

Fiona dug out her lip balm and smoothed it over her lips. "Talia, what don't you like about the dress you're in besides the neckline?"

"It's boring with a capital 'B.'" She extended her hands

outward in exasperation. "A little drama or color wouldn't hurt."

Fiona pushed through ten more options on the rack. She held up a red dress with a loud, floral skirt. "Is this colorful enough?"

Talia looked at her as if she'd grown nine heads. "You've got to be kidding. I'd look like a garden."

"Okay, I'll take that as a no." She chuckled and shoved the dress back in place.

Talia stomped back to the rack and dug through the selections. She withdrew a form-fitting cocktail dress. "Lookee here. This is more like it."

"It's very pretty, but it wouldn't pass the dress code for modesty. Too tight and the sides are covered in a lacey see-through mesh. Sorry."

Talia almost uttered a curse word, but caught herself. She mumbled something about living in the United States and not the Middle East.

"I know all this modesty stuff may seem strange, Talia, but it isn't about hiding your beauty. It's about how you handle it. Pick a dress that shows you know how valuable you are."

Talia's brows drew together as if Fiona were speaking a foreign language. From what Mom Cat had said about the clothes Talia had come with, she doubted the teen had ever had a lesson on valuing oneself or on modesty. She was probably thinking, "These people are stark raving mad."

Little lessons. According to Mom Cat, they were the key, and she'd reminded Fiona of that when she'd taken the girls with her after church services. Little lessons were what Mom Cat had given Fiona regularly, rather than long lectures. Her brief talks had left Fiona pondering the thought, rather than feeling as if she'd been hammered with Mom Cat's opinions. She hoped little lessons worked with Talia too, but she wasn't so sure.

Solana came out of the dressing room in the coral dress, flashing a broad smile. She held the sides of the skirts out and twirled. "This is it!"

"*Muy hermosa*, Solana." Fiona studied the dress. "And the fit is excellent."

"*Sí*, and it's on sale. Half price." She flipped her thick, raven-wing hair with her hand.

"You look terrific and it's perfect for you. Now, we have to find one for Talia." Fi looked around the boutique. They seemed to have exhausted the racks for teen girls. Fiona's gaze settled on a mannequin dressed in what could be "the one." The ivory skirt and mocha bodice embellished with beads would look amazing with the girl's golden-brown skin. And the neckline was modest as well. "Talia, what do you think about this dress? Do you like it?"

Talia shrugged. "Yeah, but we both know if it's on the manne-quin, it's too pricey."

Fiona fingered the price tag. "Actually, it's in the allotted price range. Is this your size?" She tilted the tag so Talia could see.

Talia nodded.

"Then, it looks like God is smiling on you. Let's get a clerk to help us. We've got a dress to try on."

The clerk wasn't a bit happy about undressing the manne-quin, but Fiona refused to be deterred. She even offered to remove the dress herself. Reluctantly, the clerk did as she was asked.

When Talia re-appeared, Fiona wanted to cheer. Even the dour-faced teenager couldn't keep a smile from blossoming on her face.

"How do you feel?" Fiona asked.

"Beautiful. Like an angel."

Solana clasped her hands together. "And you look like one, too."

"I couldn't agree more." Fiona pushed up from the chair. "Two dresses down and shoe shopping to go."

"Shoes, too?" Talia's eyes glistened.

Ah, had Fiona just found the girl's Achilles heel? She smiled at the young ladies. "Go change. I hear shoes calling your names."

Rainclouds rolled across the sky, putting Gabe's bike ride with his brother into question. "Feel like riding in the rain."

"You know I hate that." He glanced at his watch. "Spin class at the Y starts in half an hour."

"Better call and make sure there's room." Gabe pulled out his phone and placed the call. They were in luck. There were two spots left.

Twenty minutes later, they pulled up that the YMCA and made a mad dash through the rain to get to the cycling class. This thirty-minute class was followed by thirty minutes of strength training.

In the cycling room, Gabe changed from his street shoes to his workout shoes in record time. "Come on, old man."

"After Mom's post-church dinner today, I'm still not sure I can move." Chip tied his laces before they hurried to the stationary bikes and slipped their feet into the straps on the pedals.

Their teacher introduced herself as Kimmy. She was a peppy little thing who talked to them about having a mission before she began. She got them all on the same pedaling rhythm and soon had the music blaring and their heart rates pumping as they rode.

After a brief warm up, Gabe turned up the resistance on his cycle. Kimmy warned them they were going on their first ten second sprint. "Ready. Go."

Gabe dug in and pedaled hard, aiming for the one hundred twenty revolutions per minute, or RPMs, as Kimmy had suggested. "Sit back in the saddle now. Keep your shoulders down and head up. Thirty-five seconds now until your first hill."

He sat back as told, then prepared for the "hill" Kim was taking them on. He stood as directed on the pedals and pumped to the rhythm. He glanced at Chip beside him and saw a sheen on his face and arms. After a few more seconds, Kimmy led them on the next micro-interval.

Riding on a stationary bike wasn't nearly as enjoyable to him as being outside, but at least he could get an intense workout in a short amount of time. The problem with stationary bikes was that one worked really hard to go nowhere.

Is that what last night was like? The whole day had been great, but he'd had to work so hard to get Fiona to let him into her life. Afraid to scare her off, he hadn't even kissed her goodnight. Was he working hard on a relationship that was going nowhere?

The repeated sets of forty seconds of easier riding paired with the twenty seconds of hard riding didn't seem too hard until they'd been doing it for nearly twenty minutes. By then, his arms ached and the muscles in his legs burned.

Gabe mopped his brow and resumed working. Last night, she'd opened her heart to him as much as she could. But would she ever be able to fully let him into her life? Even though it would hurt to end things now, maybe it would be better for both of them.

"Come on, everyone, we're nearly there. No thoughts about quitting. It's worth it." Kimmy finally yelled. "The line's in sight. Keep pushing. Don't give up now. Three, two, one. You made it!"

Gabe leaned back in his seat and took a swig of water. He needed to take Kim's advice and not give in to thoughts about quitting. Everything about Fiona, from her sense of humor to the way she made him feel every time she looked at him, made his heart race as if he were back climbing a "hill" on the bike. The line was in sight, he was almost there, and Fiona was certainly worth it.

Fiona had never seen so many shoes. Between Solana and Talia, she figured their goal was to try on every pair in the store. Solana had wondered off, but Talia remained near.

"I like these a lot." Talia twisted her ankle to show off the rhinestone encrusted shoes in champagne satin.

Fiona grinned. Finally a keeper. "They would match your dress extremely well. You've got a good eye."

Talia sat down beside Fiona on the bench. "What's got you all happy today? It's like you're glowing or something. Hot date?"

Fiona stiffened and bit her lip. Where had this come from? Was she really acting differently? Her therapist always said cultivating transparency was part of every relationship, but did that include opening up to a troubled teenager?

She looked into Talia's eyes and saw that the girl was making a genuine, if awkward, attempt at connecting, and if she shut her down now the chance might be lost forever. "I did have a date yesterday."

"From all the grinning you did today, it must have been a good one." She unbuckled her shoe.

"I had a great time. We spent the day at the sponge docks in Tarpon Springs."

Talia's head popped up. "Who's your boyfriend? Spongebob?"

Fiona laughed. "His name is Gabe, and he's not actually my boyfriend, but we had a great time."

Talia slipped on her own shoes. "Are you going to see him again?"

"We work together, so yes."

"That's not what I meant." She met Fiona's eyes. "Will you go out with him again?"

Warmth pooled in the pit of Fiona's stomach at the thought. "Yes, if he asks."

"You think he'll ask?"

"I do." Fiona gathered up some of the boxes to return to the shelves.

"If you're lucky, maybe he'll actually take you someplace fun next time like a graveyard." Talia's eyes sparkled at her own sarcastic cleverness. She was quiet for a minute as she stuffed her shoe selection back into the box. "Does he know about you being a foster kid?"

Fiona shifted her stack and met Talia's dark eyes. "He does."

"And he doesn't mind?"

"No." Fiona heard the unasked question in the girl's voice. "He's a good man, Talia. I can trust him."

Fiona re-shelved three boxes, but Solana came round the corner with four additional pairs to try on.

"What are you looking at?" Solana pulled out a strappy pair

of silver heels. "You know what they say, 'Cinderella is proof that shoes can change your life.'"

Fiona gave Solana a side hug. "In that case, maybe I need a pair, too."

Talia raised her eyebrows. "I think you might've found your Prince Charming already."

As she drove the two girls home, Fiona thought about the progress she'd made with Talia today. Either Talia was very observant or she had a sixth sense because Fiona certainly didn't think she'd been acting differently. She sucked in her cheeks and realized that, even now, she was indeed smiling and her cheeks hurt. She shrugged. Perhaps she had been smiling a bit more than usual.

Seeing Gabe on Monday added yet another good reason to love her job.

Freshly showered and changed after the workout, Gabe sat down on a bench in the locker room and pulled out his street shoes.

Organ music piped through Chip's phone from an eerie vampire movie. Why did he have such a bizarre ringtone? Chip answered the call and grabbed his duffle. "Come on. That was Mom. We need to go."

Gabe tied his shoe and hopped up. "What's wrong? Is Dad okay?"

"Nothing's wrong." He broke into a wide grin. "We've got a new niece to meet. Ellen just had her baby."

Gabe trailed Chip to his car and climbed into the passenger

side. Gabe seldom got to drive when the two of them were together. Chip considered his law enforcement career to be the definitive reason he should always be behind the wheel. He swung the car out of the parking lot so fast Gabe had to grab the handle above the door.

"I'd like to live long enough to meet my new niece." Gabe adjusted his position in his seat.

"Yeah, you do have more to live for now." Chip eased up on the speed.

"What are you talking about?" Gabe turned on his brother's radio. A familiar romance song played quietly.

"You must have taken that pretty Child Life lady out. You've got that post-date look on your face." He glanced over at his brother.

"How did you know?"

"I didn't, but I'm a trained investigator and that whole cue ball noggin of yours blushes when you're embarrassed. Besides that, you just left 'Rewrite the Stars' playing on the radio and showtunes are not your usual choice." He stopped at the light. "I'd ask if you were planning on taking her home to meet your parents, but you already did that."

Gabe stared out the window.

"She's really something, Gabe. I think she'll be good for you."

"I didn't propose. It was one date. We spent Saturday together."

"The whole day? And she didn't dump you by the end? I think we can consider that something to mark in the plus column." He passed a car and got back in the right lane before glancing over at Gabe. "Are you having second thoughts?"

"Not really. She's amazing in so many ways, and life is never boring with her around."

"But boring is much easier to plan for, isn't it? Your modus operandi."

"I'm not boring." Gabe glowered at Chip and changed the song on the radio.

"You're not exactly Mr. Excitement either." He checked his rearview mirror. "I'm not criticizing you. It's just that you've never been a real risk-taker, that's all."

"I take risks. I have twenty-five percent of my portfolio in high-risk, diversified investments."

"That's money, and you know all the nuances of the playing field. You understand and accept that risk. If something fails, you lose money, but it doesn't cost your heart anything. That's how life has gone for you. You see something you want, and you work to get it."

"And what's wrong with that?"

"Relax. I'm on your side, and there's nothing wrong with it. It's worked well for you." He pulled into the hospital parking lot and found an open spot. He pushed up the gear shift, then gripped the steering wheel. "But falling in love is a whole new ballgame. Love is always risky. You're putting your heart out there, and she could throw it back in your face and there's nothing you can do about it." He paused and grinned. He turned to Gabe and batted his eye lashes. "Or you two could 'Rewrite the Stars.'"

Gabe opened a door and climbed out. "We better hurry. I need to get to the gift shop."

Chip followed suit. "You getting something for the baby?"

"No, I need to get a sympathy card for your wife." He gave him a mock scowl. "I don't know how Maria puts up with you."

Deep down, though, he knew Chip had hit the nail on the head. This thing with Fiona was risky, but it was too late for him to turn back even if he wanted to, which he did not. For once in his life, he didn't want to weigh the options. He wanted to do what felt right. He wanted to take long walks on the beach with Fiona McGrath, and he wanted to bring Fiona to meet the newest member of his family.

CHAPTER 19

Fiona arrived at her office door and stopped short. Why was her door ajar? Was Shannon back?

She carefully nudged it open with her foot. Stepping inside, she scanned the room. Nothing looked amiss or at least not any more amiss than it had on Friday.

Buttons wriggled his nose in her direction. Where had he gotten a carrot?

She turned to set her things down on the desk and sucked in her breath. In the center of her desk was a basket holding a loaf of homemade wheat bread. A note was tucked beside it. She tore open the envelope and read it. Gabe was making good on his claim to be a good cook. He said this was just a sampling of what he'd make for them on Saturday if she agreed to join him for a beach picnic.

When she reached for the plastic wrap, she discovered that the bread was still warm. Had he gotten up at five to make it? She breathed in the yeasty scent. He'd included a tub of whipped butter and orange marmalade. Another plastic bag was set beside it containing her chocolate-covered baklava from their date. She set that aside and prepared a slice of bread with both butter and marmalade. It was so fresh it melted on her tongue. Wow, she could get used to Monday mornings like this.

She noticed that the note had a post script on the back. "In case you need a joke of the day: Why doesn't bread like hot weather? Things get toasty."

She lowered herself into her chair and stared at the offering before her. What a gift this was. Not only did he give her the labor of his hands, he'd also given her the gift of his time. And he'd thought of everything—the butter, the marmalade, the baklava, the...carrot! When she left Buttons on Fridays, she'd provide him with ample alfalfa, and enough veggies for two days. Buttons always had all the veggies polished off by Monday morning, but the one he was nibbling on now was fresh and still had a green top attached. It had to have come from Gabe as well.

If the way to child life specialist's heart was through her therapy rabbit, Gabe Cavenaugh was certainly making headway.

She stole a few moments to eat a second piece of the sweetened wheat bread. She thought she detected a note of molasses in it. If she didn't step away soon, she was going to eat the entire loaf in one sitting.

Usually, her Monday ritual was fairly well set. After checking on the events of the weekend in the pediatric ward, she'd start with her assessments of each child.

She re-covered the bread with the plastic wrap and tucked the note in her pocket. She'd call him later and thank him, but right now, she had work to do. Child Life services didn't happen on their own.

She took a step toward the door and stopped. It was the first Monday of February. The day the hospital's board of directors met, and the day Gabe was going to recommend that the Child Life Department be cut. The bread suddenly felt like a lump in her stomach, and her loyalties were torn in shreds. How could he do this after everything he'd seen?

She touched the note in her pocket. Could she separate Gabe, the assistant chief financial officer, from Gabe, the man who made her fresh bread and brought carrots for her rabbit? On Saturday, she had thought she could, but now her emotions swirled. She felt like a traitor to her kids and to Gabe at the same time.

Blinking back tears, she bowed her head. *Lord, give me wisdom. You know this situation appears impossible. I want to believe Your promise that You'll work out everything for good. I'm trying to trust You. Please, help my unbelief.*

She took a deep breath and pressed her shoulder blades together. Whether she fretted or not, Gabe would submit his recommendation. He had a job to do and so did she—at least for a few more months.

Gabe had agonized over his decision, but he had to do what he felt was the right thing. If he didn't, he wouldn't be the man who was capturing her heart.

The file folder under Gabe's arm seemed as if it were made of concrete. He entered the board room and drew near one end of the long table. It was surrounded by at least a dozen chairs in which the hospital's board of directors and chief officers sat chatting until the meeting was officially called to order. Water bottles stood at each place like little sentries and several members had computers out and open.

He glanced across the table at his boss, the chief financial officer himself, Mr. William Case. Two weeks ago, he'd been pleased that Case wanted him to do the honor of writing the proposal to cut the Child Life Department. Today, he felt as if he were making the most difficult decision of his career.

The board president sat up straight in her leather chair. "If I can have your attention, we'll get things started." She waited while everyone swiveled their chairs in her direction. After she'd had the secretary read the old minutes, she pressed on. "On the agenda is the approval of the proposed budget for next year, and I know we all have a lot of questions. Mr. Case has been working closely with the budget committee and, as I understand it, our assistant CFO, Gabe Cavenaugh, has been tasked with figuring out how to deal with a shortfall in the operating fund. I'd like start with Mr. Cavenaugh giving us his proposal."

Gabe stepped to the front open space at the end of the table. "I don't have to tell you all that hospitals are complicated entities. We must balance quality care and financial responsibility. To do that we sometimes have to choose between what is good and what is best. What I have to recommend falls into that particular category."

He withdrew the pages he'd copied for the board from his folder. "As most of you are aware, a few years ago, Mrs. Beacher and Mrs. Wintersmith secured a grant to begin a child life program at our hospital. The grant covered start-up costs of the program and the child life specialist's salary completely the first year. The second year, it paid for half of her salary and the majority of the program's costs. By the third year, this coming year, we were to be able to take on the entire cost of the program and cover her salary."

He paused and glanced at Case. He nodded his approval, which turned Gabe's stomach. Gabe swallowed. "Two weeks ago, this would have been a much easier presentation to make because, to be honest, I had no idea what the Child Life Department did. Since then, I've shadowed Fiona McGrath, our child life specialist, and have seen how beneficial her program is to our most vulnerable patients, our children, and their families. In this day and age when quality care is paramount, personally, I feel this program is important to our work here at Bryce Memorial." The two women who'd written the original grant beamed at him.

He looked at each of the board members encircling the table. "Since the Child Life Department, however, it is not a billable program, it is difficult to put a value on the services and, worse, it's impossible to recoup the money spent. As I said, a hospital often has to give up what's good for what's best. We have a shortfall which must be made up somewhere and the cost of the Child Life Department equals that amount. Being financially stable is truly what's best for our hospital." Another quick look at Case let him the know the man was pleased with his words. "I came in here today fully ready to recommend that the Child Life Department be cut from our budget entirely, but I'd like to propose something else."

William Case glowered at him, but the two women who'd submitted the original grant proposal leaned back in their chairs.

"The budget cannot be approved in its entirety until next month's meeting. I would like to suggest that the budget submitted today will stand, including the termination of the Child Life Program, unless I am able to find alternate funding for it by the time our next meeting takes place."

Gabe kept his eyes fixed downward as he returned to his seat. Conversation buzzed around him, but he found it hard to hear the words over the thudding of his heartbeat.

William Case was most likely livid. He didn't even have to look up to feel his growing wrath. Before today, Gabe hadn't dared to disappoint the man, so he had no idea what kind of retaliation he could expect. Would he be demoted or relegated to boring tasks? Or could he even lose his job altogether?

After other budgetary discussions and a few questions directed toward Case and toward Gabe, the board finally agreed to Gabe's proposal, the budget was tabled, and the meeting concluded.

Gabe made a break for the door, hoping to avoid Case, but the man came up beside him and growled, "My office. Now." Then, the man turned to the board member next to him and, with saccharine sweetness, thanked him for his hard work on the budget committee. Maybe Case wasn't as furious as he thought he might be.

As soon as Gabe closed the office door, Case was in his face. "What do you think you were doing in there? I told you to get this done, not stir up their sensibilities. I thought I could count on you." He pointed at Gabe's chest.

Gabe took a step backwards. "Sir, I had to use my best judgement."

"You're a kid. You'd don't have good judgement!" Case's chest heaved. "And after your little speech, they're going to have a hard time cutting that idiotic, hand-holding program."

Gabe's own anger flared. "Do you even know what Fiona McGrath does? Those kids come in here hurt, sick and scared, and she makes it bearable. In my opinion, her program shouldn't be cut. She should get a raise and we should hire another child life specialist just like her."

He and Case locked eyes, neither willing to back off their position. Finally, Case walked around to his desk chair and sat down with a thud.

Gabe unclenched his jaw and rubbed the back of his neck. He had to reign this in. "Sir, I understand the deficit in the proposed budget. All I wanted was a chance to look for an alternative way to meet the shortfall."

Case slammed a fist on his desk. "If there was a way, don't you think I would have found it?"

"Probably, but there's a possibility you missed something. I think we can both agree that I'm more motivated to find it than you might have been."

Still red-faced, Case glared at him for several long seconds. "If I find out you've taken a minute from your regular duties to look into this, I—"

"I get your point, sir." Gabe nodded. "And I'll keep you informed."

"Don't bother. Your time in this department will most likely be coming to an end soon."

The air whooshed from Gabe's lungs and the room swam before his eyes. Gabe took hold of the chairback in front of him. "Sir, I hope you'll reconsider, but that's your decision."

"It sure is, Cavenaugh. No one crosses me—ever."

Keeping his head high, Gabe turned and strode from the room. What was Case's problem anyway? It wasn't like he'd made his boss look foolish. He'd only asked for more time to look at the situation. But Case wanted him to be a "yes man" and that wasn't what he'd gotten.

The weight on Gabe's chest grew heavier with each step down the hallway. Was he truly going to lose his job? Had he risked everything for Fiona McGrath and her Child Life Department?

CHAPTER 20

Fiona read the notes on the computer screen at the nurses desk about Alexis, the sixteen-year-old amputee. The notes indicated that Alexis was struggling with the new label, and Fiona understood why. How strange it was that people thought of others with one-word labels as if it summed up the entirety of the person. The amputee. The doctor. The foster child. She was as guilty of doing it as anyone else, but she knew better. While being a former foster child was part of her story, it wasn't the whole novel, and while being an amputee was now part of Alexis's story, it didn't tell what the young woman's dreams were or reveal her God-given talents. It simply labeled a chapter in her life.

After signing out on the computer, Fiona walked down the hall to Alexis's room. She found the young woman sitting up in bed with her hair brushed, a laptop positioned on her tray table, and her stump propped on a pillow. "Stump" was an ugly word, and she wished the medical personnel had something else to call the appendage.

"Good morning, Alexis. You're looking fresh today. Feel like playing a game of Blink?"

She stepped around to see what Alexis was viewing on the computer. An attractive blonde, standing on one leg and using a crutch, addressed an audience on a video.

Fiona leaned close. "Who's that?"

"My new inspiration. Her name is Caroline Larsson Mohr. She's from New Zealand, and I read about her on the internet and searched out her videos. She was big into golf, and played her first golf game on one leg just two months after her amputation. She wanted to be pro, then she got cancer and they had to remove her leg. She said her whole world crashed just like mine, but she had three weeks to prepare before her surgery."

"And you sure didn't."

"No. The psychologist says to give myself time and space to come to terms with everything because time is the real healer, but I want to get back to my life. I'm sixteen. I need my friends. I need to have fun. I need to dream about my future."

Fiona nodded and pulled out her tin containing the Blink cards. "All that makes complete sense to me. Have your friends been up here?"

Alexis shrugged. "The cheerleaders stopped by, but I could tell this—" She pointed to the stump. "—creeps them out." She closed the lid on the laptop. "Can you set this on the couch?"

Fiona did as she was asked and adjusted the tray table so they could both reach it. She dealt the Blink cards. "Do you remember how to play?"

Alexis grinned and raised the head of her bed. "They took my leg, not my brain."

Fiona flipped the three cards in the middle, then set up her draw pile and placed three cards in her hand. Alexis did the same. On "go," the two competed to get rid of their draw piles by rapidly placing cards on the piles in the middle.

"Ah!" Fiona gasped when Alexis beat her to putting a card with one green moon on a card with one brown flower. Since cards could be matched by number, color, or shape, the possibilities were endless.

"Done!" Alexis held up her hands in victory. "Ready for a rematch?"

"Absolutely. I can't leave in disgrace." Fiona gathered up the cards and shuffled.

Since each round lasted less than two minutes, they were able to complete several rounds. When Fiona saw Alexis's energy waning, she told her she needed to go. She gathered the playing cards, dropped them in the tin, and clicked the lid shut. "When you're looking up videos next time, try one about Patience Beard. She's an amputee who was also a cheerleader for the University of Arkansas."

"Really?"

"Yep. She did stunts and everything." She put her cards in her bag. "And Alexis, why don't you write to that Caroline Mohr? Tell her you're a fan."

"I might do that." Alexis nodded her head in the direction of the door. "And speaking of fans, it appears that one of yours has found you."

Fiona turned and smiled at Gabe. She hadn't seen him since Saturday, and they hadn't crossed paths yesterday or today. Even though she was dying to ask him about the board meeting, she hadn't allowed herself to contact him. She had, however, sent him a text message thanking him for the bread and baklava. She'd sent a second text with a photo of Buttons gnawing on the carrot.

She joined Gabe in the hall. "Hi, stranger."

"Hi, yourself." He fell in step beside her and waited at the computer station while she charted a few notes about her visit. "Are you off for the day?"

"I am. I just need to stop by my office." She looked at him.

"Is something wrong?"

"No." He sighed. "Long day, and I just need some help buying a baby gift."

"Your sister?"

"Had a girl. My first niece and I have no idea what I'm doing when it comes to girls."

She laughed. "Babies are babies. They eat. They sleep. They poop. Then, they repeat the whole kit and kaboodle. But I'll be glad to help you navigate the scary pink section of the big box store." They reached her office. "Hey, are there any of our cookies left from Hallas?"

"What do you think?"

She flicked a crumb off his dress shirt. "You ate the last one before you came up."

"Has anyone ever told you how brilliant you are?" He flashed her a grin.

"Good try." She went inside and grabbed her purse. "I do hope this shopping adventure involves food. I missed lunch."

"Doesn't everything I do involve food?" He placed his hand on her back. "I was thinking baby back ribs, baby carrots—"

She moaned and hit the Down button on the elevator. "I can't believe I'm saying this, but I've missed you, Gabe Cavenaugh."

Gabe had missed Fiona too. As they'd driven to the shopping center, he'd considered telling her about the meeting and all that had transpired, but he didn't want to risk ruining their time together.

They approached the doors, and they swished open. Gabe

snagged a cart.

She led the way toward the baby section and stopped when she reached the area. "What are you thinking? Clothes, toys, accessories?"

He held up his hands in surrender. "I can honestly say I am not thinking of anything."

"Did your sister sign up on the baby registry? Does her nursery have a theme?"

He chuckled. "You might as well be speaking Greek. In fact, I'd have a better chance of understanding Greek than what you're saying."

Fiona scrunched her brows. "Do you have a budget?"

"Would a hundred dollars or so cover it?"

"Why don't you just pay for a year of college while you're at it?" Shaking her head, Fiona walked toward the display racks. "I think we'll start with things that are good for the baby's development. What's her name, by the way?"

A huge smile reached his eyes. "Gabrielle."

"After you?"

"Not officially, but I can sure claim it. It wasn't like they could name her after Chip." He picked up something that looked like a mitten with a cactus hat. He wriggled two fingers inside it. "What is this?"

"A teething mitt." She picked up a set of outlet protectors.

"Does Gabby need one?"

"She will in a few months, but—"

He tossed it in the cart. "What else? How about this fishbowl thingy?"

"That's a great toy for when she's about six months. That's

when children start to get into container play. I think we can find something that better fits a newborn." She perused the selections and selected a Black, White, and Bright Floor Mirror. "This is perfect. Babies love to look at faces and this encourages tummy time."

"Tummy what?"

"Tummy time." She placed her hand on his stomach. "Babies spend a lot of time on their backs sleeping and in car seats, so parents have to make sure they get tummy time to strengthen their muscles for crawling."

"How'd you get so smart?"

"Child life specialist, remember? I studied child development."

"Got it." Gabe took the mirror set from her and popped it into the cart. "Now, this is perfect. It reminds me of you. All we need is a little crazy hat for Gabby to wear."

She turned to see that he'd found a scooter with a face on the front. The box said it could be used at three different stages. "It's adorable but she can't use it until she's at least a year old."

Gabe frowned. "Can't they hold on to it for her?"

"Do they have a big house? If they don't, it might be hard."

He set the scooter back on the shelf.

She looped her hand in the crook of his arm. "Let's look at clothes. Every mom likes to get those."

Gabe soon learned he knew nothing about onesies, sleepers, swaddle wraps, or wearable blankets, but he told Fiona to put one of each in the cart.

Fiona leaned over the cart. "I think you've got a nice gift here, Gabe."

"Don't I need a dress? She's a girl after all." He moved toward a rack and took off a dress with a fluffy tutu. How's this?"

"Fine if she was four." Fiona turned him toward the correct rack. "Pick one from this zero- to three-month section."

"Any of them?"

She hiked her shoulders. "Sure. They're all cute."

He flipped through the tiny selections of shimmery gold, bright pink, and lemon yellow. He pulled out an ice blue dotted dress trimmed in white fur. It had a tiny matching white fur jacket vest with a white satin bow in the center. He held I up. "Would this work?"

"It's perfect. Ellen will love it." She squeezed his hand. "Now, I'd like to pick out something for the baby."

He started to push the cart toward the checkout. "Why? Isn't this enough? I planned on it being from both of us. I want you to meet Gabby tonight."

"Me?"

"Yes, Fiona, you." He stopped and smiled down at her. "Don't overthink it. I'm going to need help carrying all this."

Arms loaded with gift bags, Fiona followed Gabe up the steps to Ellen and Michael's small, pale yellow house. Two hanging plants framed the front door which had been painted robin's egg blue. Gabe rang the doorbell and Fiona bit her lip.

He glanced at her. "You look nervous."

"I am."

The door swung open and Michael welcomed them in. Even

though the house was small, Fiona immediately noticed it had been renovated with laminate flooring and fresh creamy paint.

A tiny cry sounded from the next room and Michael smiled. "Ellen and the baby are in the living room as I'm sure is obvious. Can I get you both something to drink?"

Gabe looked at Fiona, who shrugged. "Two waters?"

"Got it." Michael turned. "Go ahead and go in."

Fiona followed Gabe and stood back and watched him greet his sister. After a minute or so, he turned toward Fiona. "Ellen, you remember Fiona?"

"Yes, she works with kids at the hospital, right?" She motioned to the couch. "Please, sit down."

"Open your gifts." Gabe's eagerness was like a child at Christmas.

"Brother dear, my hands are full at the moment. Do you want to take her?"

He held his hands up in front of his chest. "No, I'll pass."

"Fiona?"

"I'd love to. Can I wash my hands first?"

Ellen gave her a brilliant smile. "Yes, and thank you. So many people don't think of that with a new baby, then it's awkward when I ask them to. The bathroom's right there." Ellen pointed to a room off the hall.

When Fiona returned, Ellen was already standing and handed baby Gabby to Fiona.

"Don't let Gabe tell you I named her after him, even if she is as bald as him." Ellen told her. "I just liked the name."

Fiona laughed. "She's beautiful. Congratulations."

"Fi, come sit down so she can open the presents." Gabe took the glasses from Michael and set them on coasters.

After Fiona was seated, she looked down at Gabby's round face. She held up a finger to Gabby's fist and watched as the baby gripped it. What was it about babies that turned a woman into goo?

She tore her gaze away to watch Ellen dig into the gifts. The last bag Gabe let her open was the dress. "Oh, Fiona, this is so sweet! Thank you!"

"She didn't pick it out. I did." Gabe's bottom lip stuck out in a mock pout.

Fiona patted his arm. "He really did. I just pointed him to the right size."

"You did good, brother." Ellen smiled at him. "Now, Gabe, go wash your hands because I want a picture of you and your—"

"Namesake?"

"Niece."

When Gabe returned, Fiona laid the tiny baby in his muscular arms. Fiona's heart grabbed. Gabe would make a great dad. Gabby seemed so safe and secure with him. Fiona remembered feeling that way sitting in her father's lap. He'd been her hero and nothing in the world could touch her. But her hero had fallen and her world had crumbled.

She looked down at the precious baby Gabe held. She wanted the kind of family Ellen and Michael now had. She'd always thought she couldn't have it, but maybe she could. After all, why should her messed-up family keep her from having a family of her own?

CHAPTER 21

Each department would need to be examined and every purchase scrutinized.

Gabe stared at the numerous spreadsheets and reports he'd asked his office assistant, Gerri, to print. They were scattered across his dining room table, since he wasn't supposed to touch this topic at work. But the more time he spent with Fiona, the more important it became for him to find a way to save the Child Life Department. It meant the world to her and, every day, she meant more and more to him.

The doorbell rang and he went to the door. He opened it wide. "Chip? What are you doing here? Is something wrong?"

"Yeah, you stood me up."

Gabe hit his hand on his forehead. "We were supposed to meet for a ride, weren't we? I'm sorry. I completely spaced it off."

"It's okay. I rode anyway. Mind if I get a bottle of water from your fridge?"

"Sure. Go right ahead." Gabe stepped out of the way.

"I didn't mind the time to think," Chip called from the kitchen, before meeting Gabe in the dining room. "I've got a murder case I'm trying to wrap up."

Gabe shoved a pile of papers out of the way and told his brother to have a seat. "What's the case?"

"A cold case, actually. We were able to use national ancestry database to identify a perpetrator. The man died in prison over a dozen years ago, but at least it will bring closure to the family.

Just a girl who took a ride from the wrong man." He gulped down half the bottle.

"Wow. Talk about bad choices."

"Speaking of bad choices, what's all this? Are you bringing this much work home from the office? That's going to have a negative impact on your love life, or are you doing it for the love of your life?"

"Fiona and I aren't there, but yes, this does have to do with her program. I'm trying to find a way to save it. Surely, the hospital is overspending somewhere and we've missed it."

"How's Case feel about your scavenger hunt? I'd hate for you to put your career in jeopardy."

"Well, big brother, that ship has sailed." Gabe exhaled and explained what happened at the board meeting. "It was only a matter of time before Case and I butted heads. I won't be his or anyone else's puppet."

"Does Fiona know you put your job on the line for her?"

"Not for her, for the Child Life Department, and the answer is no. And I have no plans to tell her."

Chip finished off the water. "Take it from me. Tell her. No woman likes that kind of surprise." He patted the papers. "Good luck with all this."

"You could help. After all, I know you can add."

"And I chose law enforcement because math bored me to tears. Besides, you're looking for a needle in a haystack, like a department that spends too much on latex gloves."

"Vinyl. Too many people are allergic to latex, so we use vinyl." He grinned. "Fiona told me."

"Got it." He looked at his watch. "I'd better get a move on.

I'm taking my wife out tonight. We got a sitter and everything."

Gabe walked him to the door. "Have a good time, and I'm sorry for forgetting our ride."

Chip chuckled. "Little brother, you've got love on the brain. I can't fault you for being human."

"I'll accept your grace, but it's way too soon for me to be in love."

"There is no right time to fall in love, brother. It just happens."

After Chip left, Gabe sat back down at the table. He wouldn't call what he was feeling toward Fiona "love," would he? You couldn't fall in love with someone in the short time he'd known her. It didn't make sense.

He shook his head and dug back into the spreadsheets. He didn't have time to analyze his feelings. What he needed most— what she needed most—were facts and answers. Analyzing anything else would have to wait.

Arms full of groceries, Fiona attempted to both juggle the paper bags and punch in the code to unlock the outside door of her apartment building at the same time. She lost her hold on one bag and it hit the ground with a crunch. *Please, don't let that be the eggs.*

Managing to prop open the door with her backside, she gathered up the fallen items. The bread, cereal, chips, and salsa all remained intact, if a little worse for the wear. Thankfully, her apartment was the first on the right, so she should be able to make it to her door with the precariously balanced assortment.

She froze.

Her door was open. Maybe she'd just left it unlocked or the

superintendent had to go in for some reason, but what if she was wrong? Should she go in or call 911? Was someone inside?

She backed away until she hit the opposite wall. Despite her best efforts to keep the groceries in hand, they toppled to the floor. She stared at the door. If someone were still inside her apartment, they'd have heard the noise for sure.

Nothing.

Okay, she should be safe in pushing the door open at least enough to see in, right? Using her foot, she gave the door a gentle kick and gasped.

Someone had ransacked her apartment. She had a pretty good idea who that person was, but how had Shannon found her? After several deep breaths, she finally managed to dig out her phone and placed the needed calls.

Two deputies arrived in minutes and had her wait outside until they were certain no one was still in her apartment. She shivered even though the temps were warm. Anger, fear, and remorse all fought for reign over her emotions. How could this be happening again?

Gabe's Mazda came to a screeching halt in front of her place. He jumped out and vaulted up the stairs toward her. "Are you okay?" He pulled her into his arms without letting her speak.

Her trembling eased in his embrace, and she ached to stay there and forget this awful situation, but she finally gently pulled away. "Thank you for coming. I'm sorry to bother you."

He held up his hand. "I'd have been really upset if you didn't call. What happened?"

She'd briefly told him what she'd found before the female deputy came out and gave her the all clear to come inside.

Gabe looked down at the scattered groceries. "Yours?"

Fiona squatted to retrieve the items, but Gabe took her arm. "We can get them later. I'm sure the sheriff wants to know if anything is missing."

His hand remained on the small of her back as they entered. Fiona stood just inside the doorway and studied the living room. Two of her plants had been uprooted and dirt littered the gray carpet. Drawers had been pilfered through and were left open, giving the room an eerie feeling. Pillows and blankets had been thrown off the couch and some books had been strewn across the floor.

She picked up a pillow and set it on the couch, but the male deputy cautioned her not to touch anything yet. "My laptop is gone. It was on my coffee table." A dust-free rectangle on the table indicated the spot. "I don't see anything else missing in here."

"iPad?" Gabe asked.

"It was with me." She walked into her bedroom and looked at her jewelry box with all the tiny drawers ajar. She rushed over. "She didn't. How could she!"

"What?"

"I have one thing that belonged to my mother—a locket. It's gone." She swiped away the tears. If she started to cry now, she wouldn't be able to stop.

"Who do you mean by 'she'?" The male deputy raised his eyebrows. "Do you think you know who did this?"

"Let me check one more thing." Fiona walked into the bathroom. Medication, consisting of both prescription and over-the-counter bottles, littered the floor. One was missing. The valium she took for panic attacks. The same one Shannon took the last time. Now, she had to admit that in front of Gabe as well. "I think the person who broke in is my sister. She took my prescription for diazepam. I take it when I have panic attacks. I haven't used it for almost six months now, but it was here. The last time she broke into my place, that's what she took."

"Last time?" The male officer frowned.

Her stomach twisted again. "I've moved since then, and I didn't give her my address."

"But she knew where you work." Gabe put his arm around her waist and drew her close. "She must have followed you home."

"Ma'am, did you notice a car following you yesterday or today?" The female deputy handed her a glass of water.

"No, I wasn't looking. My mind was on other things, but I should have known better. I came home, then I went back out for groceries. I should have been watching. She's done this before and she showed up last week at my office and wanted to know where I lived." She glanced up at Gabe and their eyes met for a second.

Gabe took her hand and held it.

The male deputy took down Shannon's name and asked a few more questions, including Shannon's history with the law and with addiction. "Ma'am, do you keep your passport or your social security card here?"

"Yes, why?"

"Can you see if they're still here?"

Fiona went to a drawer in her dresser and rummaged through the clothes. "They're gone."

"Ma'am," he said, his voice solemn, "I'm afraid your sister may have taken more than the computer, necklace, and medication. I think she may be trying to steal your identity."

CHAPTER 22

Gabe picked up a broken pot and the plant it had once held. Fiona handed him a mixing bowl to hold the plant. Once he'd deposited it, he scooped some dirt over the roots. "Think it will live?"

"Maybe." She picked up the other plant. "Why did she do this? They're just plants. It's not like I could keep cash under them. It would get soaked."

"It might not be her, Fi." He rubbed her back.

"Deep in my soul, I know it is."

"She might not have been alone."

A fresh wave of violation swept over her and she put a hand on the wall to steady herself.

"Ma'am, we're all done here." The crime scene investigator stepped closer. "We've got photos and fingerprints. If you notice anything else missing, call the number on this card, and the officer will add it to the report." She passed the card to Fiona. "It's good you're not alone right now."

"I won't leave her." Gabe had already vowed that to himself.

"Thank you." Fiona sighed. "And I'm sorry you had to do all this tonight."

The woman smiled. "It's our job, ma'am, and just because you think it was your sister, doesn't mean it's your fault." She laid a hand on her arm. "Try to get some rest."

Gabe's brows knit together. Fiona's panic attack medication had been stolen and, as far as he knew, panic attacks were caused by stressful situations. Did she need that medication to get through this?

After the technician left, he locked the door which still had the fingerprinting dust on it. The technician said that whoever had entered had used a bump key to open the door. She'd explained that bump keys worked best on new, high-quality locks because the tumblers and cylinders moved more smoothly. She also said bumping left little or no signs of damage or tampering.

The female deputy had said that an older woman upstairs had admitted to opening the coded exterior door of the complex for Fiona's sister. She knew it had to be Fiona's sister because she looked just like her, except she was very thin. The older woman was the same one who'd admitted Ambrose the other day. So much for security panels?

Fiona began to straighten the contents of the disheveled drawers and close them one by one. Gabe went into the bathroom and gathered up the medications. He stuffed them all in the empty drawers, so Fi could straighten them later.

She turned. "It's almost like it never happened. Once I vacuum that dirt up, anyway."

"I think you should contact your credit card companies and bank accounts, just in case."

Her eyes widened. "No, don't tell me she could—"

"I don't know." He laid his hand on her arm. "Let me call my brother. He can help us out with this." He pulled out his cell phone.

"Gabe." Her eyes filled with tears. "What will your family think when they learn about my sister?"

"They'll understand. I promise."

Gabe had never heard his brother become all "cop business"

before. He prodded Gabe for information and asked for the case number. He told Gabe that he'd look into it personally, and that Fiona should call the fraud alert department of one of the credit reporting agencies. He also said Fiona should go to the Federal Trade Commission's webpage and file a recovery plan.

He explained that her sister most likely would try to open new credit card accounts in Fiona's name and this would prevent Shannon from being successful. However, she might also try to do something bigger like buy a car. Identity thieves had even been known to give their "new" name when arrested. Then, when the court date came, they wouldn't show and an arrest warrant would be issued in the "new" identity.

Chip insisted they do all of this tonight. They needed to act quickly because Shannon had the jump on them.

Gabe only gave Fiona some of the information. Fiona placed the call to the credit agency fraud alert department, her bank, and to her credit card companies. Then, she and Gabe worked together on the FTC's recovery plan.

Fiona stood and tugged his hand. "It's nearly one in the morning. You need to go home and get some sleep."

He didn't budge, a surge of protectiveness setting his jaw. "I'm not leaving. I'll sleep on the couch. Tomorrow, we'll make sure the locks get changed."

"Gabe, you can't. What would my neighbors think?"

He stood and held both her hands in his. He had to make her see reason. "If you won't let me sleep on the couch, then I'll sleep in my car, but I'm not leaving." She was trembling again, so he put his arms around her.

She looked up into his eyes, tears trailing down her cheeks.

"I mean I can't let you do this. It's my crazy life. I can't make you suffer because of it."

"Don't you know by now that your crazy is my crazy?" His lowered his lips to meet hers and tasted the saltiness of her tears.

If he could, he'd kiss her tears away forever.

CHAPTER 23

Fiona's eyes felt sandy and puffy, and one look in the bathroom mirror confirmed the latter. The scent of coffee and bacon wafted into her room. Heavenly. Last night, she asked Gabe to go home so her neighbors didn't get the wrong idea. He agreed if she let him stay for a while to make sure she didn't need him. Since she didn't relish trying to get to sleep in her violated apartment, she'd given in and presented him with a key to her apartment and the code to the exterior door of the complex. He tucked the key in his pocket, gave her a long hug, and said he'd watch television until she went to sleep.

Having him in the next room did ease her fears. Even though she believed it was Shannon who'd broken into her place, there was always a change it had been someone else. Gabe's kiss had certainly given her something to think about, which also helped.

She hopped into the shower and dressed. With her curls still damp, she joined him in the kitchen.

"Gabe, why are you wearing the same clothes? You promised you wouldn't sleep on my couch."

"Relax." He kissed her cheek and handed her a mug of coffee. "I kept my promise. I slept in my car. I wasn't leaving you without the locks being changed."

"Oh." She smiled, touched by his concern. "You should have gone home, but thank you."

"Hungry? I made a frittata with bacon and spinach." He dished up a triangle of the creation and she gratefully accepted.

"I would have made French toast, but your bread didn't handle last night's fall very well. I think one of the deputies must have stepped on it."

She took the fork he offered. "This is perfect, and you're too good to be true."

"Just scoring points before I do something stupid." He made himself a heaping plate and sat down at the table with her. "I need to stop by my apartment and shower before I go in today, so I'll go after we talk to the apartment manager about the locks."

"I can handle it." She ate a few bites, then looked at Gabe. "What do you think will happen to her if the sheriff's department catches her? I wouldn't want to press charges."

"I don't think it would be up to you now. Chip said that burglary is a felony in Florida."

Her chest tightened. "A felony?"

Gabe took her hand. "She chose to come here. It's not your fault."

"I keep thinking about why she did this? Why'd she come here? She could make a lot more breaking in somewhere else."

"I think she's angry with you because you're everything she's not. You've got your life in order. You're successful. You're happy." He stood up and set his empty plate in the sink. "That's one reason I stayed out front last night. She wants you to hurt."

"She blames me."

"She's an addict. She blames everyone but herself."

"I know I shouldn't feel this way, but sometimes I wonder why my life has been so hard." She took the last swig of her coffee, now grown cold, and pushed up from the table.

Gabe put his arms around her from behind. "You were given

this life because God knew that you're strong enough to live it."

"I think God overestimated me." She leaned her back against his solid chest and let his warmth chase some of the despair from her heart. Why was she being so melancholy this morning? She needed to snap out of it.

She turned in his embrace until she faced him. "You need to get moving, and so do I. We have jobs to get to."

"You're right, but you're forgetting something."

Did he expect her to initiate a kiss?

"Fi, it's Wacky Wednesday and you're way underdressed." He pressed a quick kiss to her lips and headed for the door with a final reminder about the locks.

Fiona locked the deadbolt behind him and wrapped her arms around herself. Her heart skipped, remembering his kisses. Gabe made her feel like she wasn't alone in the world, and that was something she'd wanted for a long time. She thanked God for blessing her. So much was going wrong in her life, but there was also so much going right.

"Cavenaugh, get in here!"

Gabe jolted at the sound of Case's roar. His heart pounded against his ribs. Was he going to be fired today?

He quickly deposited his briefcase in his office and said a prayer as he hurried to his boss's office. Inside the room, he was surprised to find Manny Medina, the graying chief operating officer. "What can I do for you, gentlemen?"

Case waved a set of papers in the air. "Do you know what

I've been dealing with all morning while you've been off doing whatever you please? I've had call after call and a slew of e-mails all protesting the cut of the Child Life Department. I told you I wanted this kept quiet."

"I didn't say anything, sir." Gabe looked from Case to Manny.

"Then, you know who did. It had to be her."

The way Case said the word *her* made Gabe want to punch the man. "I don't think she said anything. She hasn't had the time."

"And you know this because?"

"I heard she had a break-in at her apartment last night. That's all." Gabe decided the best way to handle William Case was to pretend there was no need for concern. He took a seat beside Manny.

"Sit down, William." Manny nodded towards Case's chair. "Perhaps some of the board members talked to their hospital staff friends. What's done is done. So, what did the e-mails say?"

Case thumbed through his stack. "This is from Dr. Renauld, the ear, nose and throat guy. He claims that crazy woman is actually making the hospital money. He says that every time the child life specialist sees one of his patients, he estimates the visit can save at least five minutes of time for his surgical team. If she sees ten kids, that's fifty minutes, which is time for a whole extra surgery."

Gabe leaned back in his chair. "He may have a point."

"It's preposterous." He used the papers to point to Gabe. "And I think every pediatrician we work with contacted me. There are letters from everyone from Emergency to Radiology to physical therapy. They all love her. And that doesn't even cover the parents of the peds patients."

"That doesn't sound like a problem." Manny crossed his right ankle over his left knee. "I thought you called me down here because you said we had to keep WW2 from breaking out."

Case tossed the papers down on his desk. "What we're about to have is a mutiny."

"Sir, I am still looking at the proposed budget, so we can honestly reply that we are doing our best to save the department."

"Don't you think I know how to do my job? I stay on top of everything. Nothing happens financially in this hospital that I don't know about."

Manny chuckled. "William, we both know that's impossible. Give Gabe a chance. He may find something. Isn't he your best man?"

"Was." Case's face hardened and his gaze bore into Gabe.

Gabe swallowed. "I've been working on this budget review outside of my work hours as per your request, but I think we need to take a careful look at our hospital's goals. What do we advertise? 'Outstanding care. Extremely close.' It seems to me that the patients and staff are seeing the Child Life Department as part of that outstanding care. If we cut this program, will it be a step forward or a step backwards in patient centric care?"

"Don't be a bleeding heart. The bottom line, Cavenaugh, is always what?"

"Cash is king."

"And there is not enough cash to keep this program." He glared at Gabe. "Make her stop talking."

"As I said—"

Manny stood. "Come on, Gabe. He doesn't see reason when he's like this. Let's go discuss what you've found already. Maybe

I'll think of something that you number-crunchers wouldn't consider."

Gabe followed the COO out, both energized and frustrated. Was Case's position really based on the budget or did he have a personal beef with Fiona? Or was his biggest concern looking bad in front of the board?

He drew in a long breath as he entered his office with the COO. He welcomed Manny's assistance and his support, but Case was a jealous man. Would Manny's involvement only solidify Case's decision to let him go?

CHAPTER 24

Once Buttons had finished the lettuce she'd brought him, Fiona lifted the rabbit from his Flop House and cuddled him close. She drew her hand across his warm, soft fur.

After her therapy appointment, Fiona had decided she needed some bunny time. Besides, poor Buttons hadn't received as much attention as he deserved since a certain bald man had entered her life. She'd brought a sack of empty paper towel rolls yesterday for Buttons to gnaw on. It had proved a great diversion.

She set the rabbit on the floor and watched him hop across the carpet. He loved the freedom to roam wherever he liked. When he looked at her, his nose twitched as if to say "thank you."

She sat down at her desk and surveyed her "home away from home." Every shelf and cabinet held the items she needed to do her work. Sure, it looked a bit like an explosion at a toy store, but she knew where each item was located. She released a long, slow sigh. It would be hard to leave this place. As much as she believed in Gabe, she feared he wouldn't find a solution.

Her therapist, Laura, had suggested she prepare for either eventuality, so she'd returned to her office tonight. Without a laptop, she needed to use the hospital computer to update her résumé and begin looking for job openings in Tampa.

She and Laura had talked a great deal about Gabe, as well. Laura was pleased to hear that Fiona was opening her heart to a man she apparently trusted. Gabe, according to Laura, seemed like someone who deserved her trust.

Fiona admitted that he was almost too good to be true, but Laura told her that thought was her insecurity rearing its ugly head. She gave Fiona homework to complete which included a list of verses to not only look up and commit to memory, but to also embrace with her heart and soul.

The ringtone on her cell phone played. She didn't recognize the number, but answered it anyway. It was Chip Cavenaugh. He was calling to tell her that they'd found her sister.

"Is Gabe with you now?" Chip asked.

"No, I'm at work in my office. Why?" Her pulse rate raced.

"Are you sitting down, Fiona?"

"Yes." Her voice wavered.

"Good. Shannon overdosed on fentanyl. The deputy who responded gave her two doses of Narcan, and she's in the hospital now."

"Which hospital? Can I see her?"

"No, but they said she's going to be okay. They'll book her as soon as she's released, but she's in our custody." He paused. "She was in pretty rough shape but, thankfully, one of the people in the place she was staying called 911 when her lips started turning blue."

"Oh." She felt the color drain from her face and her breath came in short gasps. *Please Lord, don't let me have a panic attack now.* She had to get off the phone. "Thank you for contacting me. I appreciate it more than you know."

"I'll keep you informed." His voice reminded her of Gabe's. "They're watching her close. Try not to worry."

After he hung up, Fiona scooped up Buttons, and her sweaty palms stuck to his coat. It was getting harder to breathe by the second. Try not to worry? Surely a member of the Cavenaugh family understood how hard it would be not to worry about a family member in the hospital.

Stop. Center yourself. Panic attacks are not life-threatening. You have survived this before and will do so again. She focused on Buttons' soft coat, using him as her anchor, as she drew in long, slow deep breaths.

She would survive. She would. She would.

Her phone rang again and she glanced at the screen. Gabe.

She ignored the call. She didn't want him to see or hear her like this—ever.

The words on the spreadsheets blurred beneath Gabe's gaze. Why hadn't Fiona answered her phone?

Chip had said she was at her office. Should he go there?

He heaved a sigh. Fiona might need some time to process all this. If he wasn't careful, he'd smother her.

Returning to work, he glanced at the list he'd been making of items that seemed out of place, like an inordinate number of light bulbs. Did fluorescent light bulbs really cost three fifty each? He could check all of the items he'd noted against the previous year's expenditures when he got to work tomorrow if he had the time. Unfortunately, Case seemed determined to keep him from looking into any of this. He'd piled on more work than ever.

His phone rang and he yanked it up. Fiona.

"Hi," she said. "Sorry, I missed your call."

Relief washed over him because she didn't sound devastated.

"Chip called and told me what was going on. I just wanted to check on you."

"I'm fine, but thank you." Her voice was soft, but it didn't sound tight as if she'd been crying.

He rubbed his hand over his bald head. "Are you really okay? How are you feeling?"

"I don't know. Scared, hurt, angry, frustrated. You name it. I guess I'm feeling it. More relief that she's been found than anything else and that she should be okay." She released a shuddering sigh.

"Maybe you shouldn't be alone." He paused. "I'm about to head over to my parents' for dinner. Want to join me? Or I could tell them I can't make it and we can go somewhere to talk."

"I think I'll take a raincheck if you don't mind. I'm not the best company. Good night, Gabe."

She hung up without letting him ask any more questions. Maybe it was still too fresh to talk about. At least he'd heard her voice for himself.

After gathering up his papers and stuffing them in his briefcase, he left for his parents' home, still feeling uneasy about Fiona. He considered going to her place anyway, but he decided against it. If she wanted to be alone, he needed to respect that. She'd survived this long without him, and she could continue to do so.

Less than twenty minutes later, he was in his mom's kitchen, watching her stir a pot of chili.

She looked at him and raised her eyebrows. "How are things going with saving Child Life?"

"I'm working on it, Mom." He grabbed a handful grapes from a bowl on the island. "I'm going through each department's expenditures, looking for over-spending we missed. I thought something would stand out, but hospitals spend a lot of money on strange things."

"Like?"

"Tylenol. We bill patients fifteen dollars a pill for something they can get at the store for ten cents. No wonder patients complain."

"That's medicine."

"And why do the emergency docs use so much Cromoxicillin?"

"I have no idea. I've never heard of that drug."

Gabe shrugged. "Must be new. Maybe that's why it's so expensive."

She motioned to the cupboard. "Get the bowls down, will you?"

He did as he was asked. "And do you have any idea how many cases of vinyl gloves surgery goes through in a week?"

"Well, son, they can't reuse them." She tasted the chili. "So how's Fiona doing? Chip told us about the robbery and about her sister. Is she all right?"

He emptied saltine crackers into a basket and followed his mother to the table. "As well as can be expected, I guess. I haven't exactly had experience with siblings with substance abuse issues, but I hate that she's going through all this."

His mother turned and stared into his eyes. "You've fallen for her, haven't you?"

"What if I have?"

"I'm happy if you're happy." She wrapped an arm around his waist and squeezed. "Just promise me you'll guard your heart and hers. That young woman can't deal with much more right now."

Gabe had to agree. As strong as Fiona was, he feared she was nearing a breaking point. Instead of worrying about her job, he needed to spend time praying for her heart to be strengthened as only God could do.

Fiona hated disappointing Gabe, but she'd called early on Saturday morning to postpone their beach date. Mom Cat had phoned and wanted her to come over for the day. She had something she wished to discuss with her. Fiona figured it had something to do with Talia.

But Gabe had still wanted to see her, so he offered to come along. She figured now was as good a time as any for him to meet her "family." She missed him, too, and her mind was still reeling from yesterday's news about Shannon. She told him if she did get to see Shannon, she wanted to be available, and he promised to take her when the time came.

She pulled her hair into a ponytail and grabbed two granola bars before rushing out the door. She passed him one bar in the car. "I figured you're always hungry, and I didn't want to have to beg for food to feed you as soon as we arrived."

"Funny lady."

"I try." She flashed him a flirty smile.

The drive was an easy one on this rainy morning. Thick, gray clouds hung over the area, and she doubted the rain would stop any time soon.

Upon their arrival, Mom Cat and Duane greeted her in the living room. Fiona introduced Gabe, and they welcomed him warmly. While she was telling them about Gabe, she noticed the kids weren't around. That was odd.

"Where is everybody?" she asked.

"The boys are back with their mom now, and the girls are in their rooms." Mom Cat studied her. "Fiona, you look tired."

She should have realized that no amount of make-up would keep Mom Cat from seeing the papery gray half-moons beneath Fiona's eyes. Gabe took her hand as she told her foster parents about the robbery, Shannon's overdose, and her subsequent arrest.

"That explains a lot." Duane looked at his wife.

The hairs on Fiona's neck prickled. "What's going on?"

Mom Cat leaned forward in her chair, her hands clasped in front of her. "Dear, your father contacted us."

"From prison? He still had your number?"

"Yes, he had our number." Mom Cat hesitated. "And honey, he's been out for six months."

"How can that be? He never contacted us."

"He did speak with your sister—and apparently, she contacted him this morning."

"I don't understand." A sickening confusion clouded her mind like a thick fog. Shannon had spoken to her father? Today?

"Apparently she's been released from the hospital and been booked. She got one phone call, and she placed it to him." Duane growled. "He called us because he wanted to know if you could help her get a good attorney. We told him you could not although we didn't even know the whole story."

"He didn't come for me." The room swam before Fiona's eyes. Her breath came in gasps. "I wrote him, all those years, but he didn't come."

Gabe wrapped his arm around her shoulders, but she yanked away. "I—I need to get out of here. I need to be alone."

She rushed from the house, out into the rain. Rivulets of water trailed down her cheeks, mixing with the tears. Rain soaked through her shirt and she prayed it would wash away the ache in her heart. She dropped to her knees on the lawn. She'd lost everyone—her mother, her sister, and now, even her father. Why hadn't he come back to her after all these years? He'd reached out to Shannon. Why not her? Deep in her soul, she knew the answer.

He didn't love her. She wasn't enough. She was never enough.

CHAPTER 25

Gabe accepted the cup of coffee from Mom Cat. She'd persuaded him not to go after Fiona for at least fifteen minutes. If Fiona didn't return by then, he could go find her. Mom Cat, however, said Fiona had always needed some time to process things before she could face everyone else.

A plaque on the wall read, "Families aren't like socks. They don't have to match." Even though this was a foster home, after meeting the Martins, he imagined this was a very special family and great home.

"May I ask you, why was Fiona's dad was in prison? I've never asked. Did he sell drugs?"

"Heavens no." Mom Cat sat down in her chair again. "Fiona was raised in a fairly well-to-do home before her world was torn apart. Her father was in real estate, and she had the best of everything—nice home, private schools, amazing toys. Her father was convicted of insurance fraud and arson and sentenced to fifteen years in prison."

That explained a lot about Fiona, but not about her father's crime. "What did he do?"

Mom Cat lifted her mug to her lips and sipped the brew. "Apparently, he purchased a lot of low value properties. Some he 'flopped.'"

"You mean 'flipped'?" Gabe asked.

"Yes, that's it." Her cheeks colored. "But others he intentionally damaged with water or fire and turned the losses in to the insurance company.

"Between the fines and restitution, Fiona's family lost nearly everything. They were allowed to keep only essentials and had to move into a tiny apartment. Her mother sunk into a terrible depression, and those two little girls were basically fending for themselves." Mom Cat swiped a tear from her eye. "Then, their mother drove her car into that concrete divider on the interstate. It's a wonder both she and Fiona weren't killed. Fiona was angry for a long time, but found healing in the Lord. Shannon did okay for a while, then she turned to drugs."

Anger flared inside Gabe for the injustice of the whole situation. A pulse throbbed in his clenched jaw. Her father's greed had hurt so many lives. He might be the only one in prison, but they were all doing the time. And now, that same man had hurt her all over again.

He couldn't wait any longer. He had to find her. Crossing the room to the window, he peered out into the backyard. She wasn't in view. He grabbed his jacket from the back of the couch, stuffed his arms into the sleeves, and hurried out the door.

He spotted her sitting on a swing. This smart, caring, resilient woman who'd captured his heart with her spirit and laughter sat with her face upturned toward the sky until she noticed him. As rain drenched his jacket, he stood there with his arms open and waited. Coming to him had to be her choice.

She looked from his extended hands to his face and slowly stood. Her internal struggle was palpable. Would she let him walk through this with her?

She hesitated, then took a few steps. Finally, she ran into his arms.

With rain soaking them both, he held her. It was nothing, and it was everything. He couldn't fix it, but he could be there.

And she didn't push him away.

A sunny Monday morning greeted Fiona when she exited her apartment. The trauma of the weekend had left her feeling numb but she had work to do. Her kids needed her.

At the hospital, she made her rounds and decided how she could serve each of the pediatric patients. She took one child to Radiology for a test and walked through it with her, and educated another child about her condition. After a quick check-in with the playroom volunteer, she made arrangements to meet with Alexis's cheer team after school to discuss how they could better support their friend after her amputation.

When the ER paged her, she finished up her game with an orthopedic patient and hurried downstairs with her purple bag. They needed her help with a fearful toddler.

After Fiona introduced herself to an agitated Ruby and her mom, she opened her Mary Poppins bag and pulled out a jar of bubbles. Ruby would have to take a deep breath in order to blow out the bubbles. She calmed as they repeated the use of the bubble wand. Before Ruby realized it, the procedure was over and she was ready to go home.

When Fiona left Ruby's room, Gabe was waiting for her at the nurses station. She tensed. Saturday, she'd been so raw, and she'd let her guard down. Sunday, still trying to be supportive, he'd joined her for church services, but what was he thinking about her today? Now, he'd had a chance to consider about her family's ugly details and secrets.

His eyes seemed to light when he saw her coming. "Hi, I was hoping to run into you. It's almost lunch. Hungry?"

"Not as much as you—ever." She gave him a lopsided grin.

"Hey, Fiona." Dr. Abrantes stood on the other side of her. "Thanks for your help. You're the best."

Gabe stepped around her. "Doc, can I ask you a question?"

"Sure."

"I've been going over some budget stuff, and I was wondering why you ER docs prescribe so much Cromoxicillin."

"What?"

"Cromoxicillin."

"I've never heard of that. Are you sure you don't mean amoxicillin?"

Gabe shook his head. "No, I'm sure it started with a 'c.'"

Dr. Abrantes shrugged. "You might check with the other docs. Maybe it's been withdrawn or something, but I don't prescribe it."

"But last year, the ER was billed nearly a hundred seventy-five thousand dollars for it."

Fiona straightened. This didn't seem right. "Carlos, isn't there some kind of drug database?"

"Sure, you can check with the DrugBank or ask Pharmacy. They'd know." He touched Fiona's arm. "Still waiting for you to accept my dinner invitation."

Gabe cocked his head.

"Sorry, Carlos, I'm unavailable."

"I'll be waiting." He flashed her a toothy grin accompanied by a wink before turning to leave.

"If I have my way, you'll be waiting forever." Gabe muttered before turning to Fiona. "I want to go check that information again. Want to meet me in my office and we'll head down for lunch?"

"Perfect. I've got one patient to see."

He brushed a kiss on her cheek and disappeared down the hall.

Fiona kept replaying the odd drug question in her head. Had Gabe possibly found something illicit? Was it someone in the ER or was it higher up? She shook her head. That was ridiculous. All the criminals in her life were making her suspicious of everyone.

Adrenaline pumped through Gabe's veins. His heart raced. There was no such drug listed on any database. He knocked on William Case's door. As the chief financial officer, he needed to know that something was awry with these charges.

Case told him to come in. Although Gabe didn't expect a warm reception, he was still not prepared for the man's abrupt change toward him which had occurred in the last few weeks. He gruffly told Gabe to have to sit down.

"Sir, I wanted you to be the first to know that I believe my examination of each department has yielded a serious discrepancy." Gabe tried to sound professional, but even he could hear the excitement in his voice.

"You were working on that today, even after I specifically said that any investigation had to be done on your own time?"

"Yes, sir, but—"

"I've had it with you. You're letting your feelings for that child life lady color everything." Case struck his fist on the desk. "That's it, Cavenaugh. You can either turn in your resignation by the end of the day, or I'll call human resources and inform them that you've been terminated."

A cold sweat broke out on Gabe's body. An earthquake couldn't have shaken him more, but he refused to give Case the satisfaction of rattling him. He drew in a deep breath and glared at the man. "I'll tender my resignation then, effective immediately. Are you interested in what I discovered? It may even involve illegal activity. Someone needs to get to the bottom of this. If I'm right, then thousands—"

"I don't think it's necessary. Anything you've found will just stir the pot more than what's already been done, and I've examined all that personally." Case picked up some papers. "Clean out your desk before you go today."

Gabe pushed to his feet, his legs trembling and his fists clenched at his sides. This was infuriating and unbelievable. Anger propelled him from the room. Beyond Case's personal gripe with him, what he'd found necessitated some kind of investigation for the hospital's sake. Was Case afraid it would make him look bad if he'd missed something?

He pressed the call button on the phone in his office and asked Gerri to have maintenance bring him some boxes. Then, he began to gather the papers strewn on his desk, including the billing statements for the Cromoxicillian.

If Case wasn't going to look into this, he and his brother would.

After playing a rousing game of hospital bed basketball with a ten-year-old, Fiona packed up her things and headed toward the door.

"Fiona." The boy repositioned his broken leg. "what's the joke of the day?"

She turned. "What's a tornado's favorite game to play?"

The boy shrugged.

"Twister."

Her patient was still belly laughing as she closed his door. She loved how children could truly enjoy the little things.

She glanced at her watch. If she didn't get a move on, Gabe would waste away.

It took only a few minutes to reach the financial offices. Whenever she stepped into this area, she always felt as if she'd left the hospital. Maybe it was the darker interior colors or maybe the loss of the sterile hospital smell, but it never quite seemed connected to the patients it served.

She leaned over the reception desk. "Hi, Gerri. How's it going?"

Gerri looked up at her and scowled, then went back to her work at her computer terminal.

Concern pricked Fiona. "Gerri, have I done something to offend you?"

Gerri spun her office chair toward Fiona. "You're ruining a good man's life. You know that, don't you? Then, you come down here all happy as if you don't have a care in the world."

"What are you talking about? How am I ruining Gabe's life?"

Gerri stood up. "You don't know, do you?"

"Know what?" Fiona's heart thundered. "Please tell me."

The office manager leaned closer. "About forty-five minutes ago, Mr. Case gave Gabe a choice to resign or be fired."

"Why? How do you know?"

Gerri hiked a shoulder. "I know everything that happens around here. And the reason was because Gabe was determined to find a way to save your program, and he discovered something."

"He found a way to save it?" Fiona rubbed her hand over her face. "Then, why did Case force him out?"

Gerri sighed, long and slow, shaking her head. "Missy, Mr. Case's main concern is first and foremost Mr. Case. Until Gabe met you, he was just fine with that. Then, you opened his eyes toward the patient side. You ruined him. This is his resignation letter. Sign, sealed, and ready for me to deliver to Mr. Case."

Fiona's mouth went dry. She backed away from the desk as tears clouded her eyes. She couldn't face Gabe now. She had to get out of there. Gabe was losing his job—a job he loved—and all because of her.

CHAPTER 26

Gabe wasn't taking "no" for an answer this time. He climbed out of his Mazda, punched in the code to Fiona's apartment complex, and knocked on her door. She didn't answer, so he used the key she'd given him to let himself in. He must have beaten her home.

She'd skipped out on their lunch, but at least she'd sent him a text saying something had come up. That was hospital life.

Even though he figured he should have felt upset by the day's events, losing his job was oddly freeing. Now, there was nothing standing in his way of looking deeper into the drug situation. He'd already phoned Chip and made plans to meet him in the morning to go over the facts he'd obtained.

He might have started out looking into this to save the Child Life Program and Fiona's position, but this had grown beyond that. It was now about what kind of man he was, what he would stand for, and what kind of person he was willing to work beside.

He heard a key in the lock. The door opened and Fiona gasped. She pressed her hand to her heart. "Gabe, you scared me to death."

"You look awfully good for a dead person." He crossed the room to welcome her. He pulled her into his arms for a long hug, which he needed more than he'd admit. "I came to kidnap you."

She pulled back far enough to look up at him. "That's against the law, and I have enough lawbreakers in my life."

"Okay, then come willingly." He kissed her forehead. "I picked up stuff for a picnic, and I have it in my car. Before you ask, of course there's chocolate, too. I thought we'd head to the beach before it got dark. I had a pretty awful day, and I wanted it to end on a high note."

She looked downward and gently pushed away. "Let me go change."

He watched her walk toward her bedroom. There was no spring in her step, no saucy glances, and no teasing words. He'd had a bad day, but her last few weeks had been unbearable. Perhaps tonight would be a turning point for both of them.

Fiona kicked off her sandals and rolled up her jeans. She stuck her feet into the damp, powder-soft sand and breathed deeply. Pure heaven.

Gabe had parked in the northernmost parking lot at the Honeymoon Island State Park. He'd suggested they walk north from there since that area was often least populated.

"Please don't tell me you're going to leave your shoes on." She pulled Gabe to a stop beside her.

He chuckled and followed her lead. They both deposited their shoes in a beach bag Fiona had brought, then Gabe picked up the picnic basket again. Holding hands, they walked along the beach. Fiona glanced back and saw their side-by-side footprints. Soon, the tide would come in and wash them away.

She licked her lips, tasted the salt from the ocean breeze, and prayed for courage. She stopped and picked up a handful of shells. An osprey glided over the waters, and then plunged feetfirst to catch a fish in its talons. The bird rose, heavy with its dinner, and flew away.

They selected a spot and Gabe pulled a blanket from the basket. Once they were seated, the two of them ate the picnic he'd brought. It was simple fare from a local restaurant consisting of fried chicken, dinner rolls, potato salad, and ooey, gooey brownies.

With his white shirt untucked and the cuffs folded to his elbows, Gabe looked more relaxed than she'd ever seen him. The rolled-up jeans didn't hurt either. He leaned back on the blanket and traced his fingers down her arm, prickling her flesh.

She loved being with him. She loved his touch. She loved the way he made her feel safe and cherished. But what did she give him?

Fiona waited for him to confide in her about what had happened with his job today, but he said nothing, and she knew why. He was protecting her. What kind of relationship could they have if he didn't feel like he could share his worst days with her?

Was she being fair? Maybe he needed more time before he talked about it or maybe she should break the ice. Her heart ached for him, but she couldn't bring herself to broach the topic. Instead, their time together was filled with discussions about her day.

When they'd finished eating, he packed up their dinner. Faint ribbons of color waved across the evening sky and the sea lapped against the shore. Since the park officially closed at sundown, they needed to start back toward the car.

Gabe stood and offered his hand to help her to her feet. She accepted and picked up the blanket. She folded it and Gabe stuffed it into the picnic basket.

Still barefoot, they retraced their steps along the beach. Gabe spotted a feather and bent to retrieve it. "You like these don't you?"

"I do. They remind me of my favorite verse—Psalm 91:4. 'He will cover you with His feathers and under His wings you will find refuge."

He stopped, set the basket on the sand, and drew her to him. He kissed her gently, long and sweet. Her insides flamed.

How had she allowed herself to fall for this caring man, who was full of integrity, humor, romance and a love for the Lord?

She wanted to promise to be his forever, but it wasn't fair to him.

"Fiona." He cupped her cheek. "I love you."

The words made her heart sing, then the sour note of truth struck. She covered his hand with her own, tears springing to her eyes. "I can't let you love me."

Gabe froze. "What are you talking about?"

She stepped away from him, focusing on the sand, rather than the pain in his eyes. "I love you too much to let our relationship keep going. I'm not good enough for you. I never have been. I wasn't enough to save my sister. I wasn't enough to bring my father back from prison. I wasn't even enough to save my job. Beneath all the jokes, there's just me, a broken clay pot. Gabe, my life is a mess. My family is mess. I'm a mess."

Gabe shook his head. "That doesn't make a difference to me. Haven't I shown you that?"

"But my mess is affecting you now, too."

"How?"

"Gabe! You lost your job today because of me!" She held out her hands to him, palms upwards, as tears flowed down her cheeks. "And that's just the beginning. My messed-up family will always be there in the shadows. My own personal demons will raise their ugly heads, and I won't put you through that. I love you too much to let you get any more involved with me."

"I'm already involved with you." Gabe ran his hand over his bald scalp, his breathing rapid. He walked away, stopped, and stared out at the ocean. He pinched the bridge of his nose and squeezed his eyes shut. After a long minute, he finally turned. "Fiona, I could stand here all day telling you that you're more than enough for me, but until you believe it for yourself, until you believe you are who God made you to be, my words mean nothing."

A park ranger waved at them. "Park's closing in five minutes. Best get to your car."

Gabe nodded to the man, picked up the picnic basket, and strode to the car. "You heard the man."

She followed his footprints in the sand, her heart shattering more with each step. *Please Lord, help him understand I'm doing this for him.*

CHAPTER 27

Another sleepless night left Gabe feeling achy and sluggish, but he was to meet with a forensic accountant from the FBI this morning, so he needed to drag himself out of bed. Gabe had discovered that the Cromoxicillin had been billed to the hospital through a company called Bioflex Pharmaceuticals. However, he could find no website for the pharmaceutical company. When he'd called Chip to share his concerns, Chip had insisted they immediately turn over the information to the FBI as it might involve healthcare and/or wire fraud, and both were federal crimes. Chip said it was imperative that everything be done right, especially in a case like this.

Gabe showered and put on his Armani suit. As he was looping his necktie, he noticed something on the lapel. He picked off one of Buttons' hairs. When had that happened? Of course, on that first fateful day when he literally ran into Fiona in the hallway. He sucked in a deep breath trying to relieve the squeezing sensation in his chest.

After putting on his shoes, he went in the kitchen and opened the fridge. Nothing looked good, and he had no appetite. He shut the door and grabbed an apple from a bowl on the table. At least it was something.

He snagged his briefcase and headed out the door for the FBI field office in Tampa. At least his new employment status gave him the freedom to do this. It would have been hard to explain his absence to Case if the man forbade him from looking into the matter further.

Gabe cranked the radio inside her car. Although the drive to Tampa usually took around thirty minutes, Gabe had given himself extra time to get there. He attempted to organize his thoughts, but Fiona kept parading through his mind. Even though he was certain about what he'd found, his nerves were frazzled by the time he pulled into the FBI parking lot. He rolled his shoulders and neck and took the time to say one more prayer.

Special Agent Reuben Kennedy came into the outer office to greet him and take him back to a conference room where they could talk. Special Agent Kennedy was a middle-aged man with wire-framed glasses and a bulbous nose. Graying hair at his temples indicated this was probably not the man's first fraud case.

Gabe brought out the paper trail he'd found and the two of them began to go over the details. Special Agent Kennedy took notes on a legal pad and asked so many questions Gabe lost track.

"From what I'm seeing, your instincts are spot on." The agent tapped his pen on the notepad. "We'll follow the hospital's money and see where it leads, but we'll need some court orders to do that. Do you think your boss will open his books without that?"

"My former boss." Gabe sighed when he saw Special Agent Kennedy's furrowed brow. "It's a long story, but the answer is no, I don't think he'll cooperate. He didn't want me to pursue this."

"Why do you think that is?"

He shrugged. "I've gone over it again and again. He was angry with me when I brought it to him over another matter. He always likes to look good to others, and this would make him look bad, and it would also call into question his supervision."

The agent made a flurry of notes. "In your opinion, could he be connected somehow?"

"I wouldn't have said so a few months ago, but he's been so odd lately, I really don't know."

"If you're not working at the hospital, you have no reason to speak to anyone there, right?"

His gut tightened at the fresh, unintentional jab. He swallowed. "No, I don't need to speak to anyone there."

"Good." He pushed back from the table and stood. He waited until Gabe also stood to offer his hand. "Thanks for coming in. Can you find your own way out? I want to get started on this."

"Sure." Gabe opened the door. "Thank you for looking into this."

Special Agent Kennedy clapped his hand on Gabe's shoulder. "No, thank you, Mr. Cavenaugh. We'll be in touch."

Fiona had taken the day off. She'd tried to function the last few days, but the weight on her heart made it nearly impossible to put on a smiling face. Besides, she'd made an appointment to visit her sister at the jail today. She'd never been to a jail before, so she'd asked Ambrose to join her. He agreed and would pick her up soon.

According to the Pinellas County Jail website, they provided visitation by video at the jail round the clock and at four different locations in the county on specific days. She opted for the jail, and decided to bring Ambrose because with approximately three thousand inmates, she thought she might run into some questionable people visiting other incarcerated loved ones.

Ambrose would be a welcome companion, but she truly wished Gabe was with her.

Her heart ached more today than it had the last time Gabe had dropped her off. How could she miss one man so much? The wound still felt as fresh as it had the night on the beach.

Ambrose arrived right on time—on his motorcycle! He held out an extra helmet. "Good, you're wearing jeans and tennis shoes. That'll work."

She shook her head. "Uh, we can take my car."

"Get on." He patted the passenger seat. "No one says 'no' to a ride on a Harley. You can sit behind me and hold on to my waist."

Her nerves grew taut, but she climbed aboard and put down the passenger foot pegs. "You sure you know what you're doing."

He chuckled and seated himself. "Have I ever?"

"That's what I'm afraid of."

"I'd never let anything hurt you, Fiona." He balanced the bike, put up the kickstand, and started the engine. "Now, hold on tight."

At first, her stomach flip flopped on every turn, but in time, a surge of exhilaration swept through her. All of her senses seemed magnified. She caught a whiff of someone's freshly cut grass, and the mouth-watering scent of grilled steaks as they passed a restaurant. She was keenly aware that there was nothing between her and the vehicles driving alongside them. Even though she'd never want to drive a motorcycle herself, she had to admit that being a passenger wasn't so bad.

They made their way toward the Pinellas County Jail and came to a stop in front of the Administrative Support Building. She took off the helmet and passed it to Ambrose.

Ambrose used helmet locks to attach the headgear to the

Harley. "I knew you'd like it."

"I did after I got my heart out of my throat." She looked at the building. "Do you know where we're going when we get in there?"

He shrugged. "I've never been on this side of jail."

They walked inside the administration building and located the Video Visitation Center. They each presented photo ID's and were directed to a cubicle with a video terminal. Other visitors populated terminals, including a mother who'd brought her children. How sad.

Ambrose said he'd remain quiet during her visit with Shannon if he could, because he knew Fiona and Shannon had things to work out. "It might take a minute. Shannon has to get to the designated terminal inside the jail before your visit can start."

Shannon's face appeared on the monitor a few seconds later. Her hair was pulled back in a ponytail, which did little to soften the sharp curves on her gaunt face. Dark circles under her watery eyes indicated exhaustion, and she offered no welcoming signs at the sight of Fiona or Ambrose.

"What are you doing here, Fi?" Shannon spat. "Sorry she dragged you along, Ambrose."

Fiona forced a smile. "I wanted to see how you were doing for myself."

"I'm peachy." Sarcasm dripped from her voice. "Why are you pressing charges? I'm your sister."

"Yes, you are my sister, but that didn't stop you from breaking into my home." She stopped herself. She did not want to lash out at Shannon. "And I'm not the one pressing charges. By attempting to steal my identity, you crossed the line and the State is charging you."

Shannon lifted a shaky hand to her forehead. "I want out of here. I am so dope sick I think I'll die."

"I know it's hard, but you won't die."

"Are you gonna get me a decent lawyer?"

"Dad said you wanted me to do that."

Ambrose leaned forward. "I can't believe you want her to put out money for an attorney, when you're charged with breaking into her apartment and attempting to steal her identity. That's ridiculous."

"Is that a no, then?"

"Yes, it's a no." Fiona dug her nails into her palms. "When did you talk to Dad, anyway?"

Shannon swiped at her runny nose. "I ran into him at his new job. He told me he was at a half-way house. He wanted to get his life straightened out before he reconnected with us."

"He didn't call you?"

"Nope."

"He didn't reach out to you?"

"With what? A Bat-Signal ?"

Fiona stiffened in her chair. "Did he say anything else?"

"Yeah, he saw Mom's locket around my neck and he asked for it. I gave it to him. Seemed fair. It wasn't mine."

"No, it was mine."

Shannon gave her a bitter smile. "And he told me to get clean before I ended up in prison or dead. Too little, too late, I guess." She fidgeted in her seat. "Listen, if you're not going to get me a lawyer, why are you here?"

"Because you're my sister. Our sister." She looked at Ambrose and he nodded. "God loves you and so do I."

"And I believe in unicorns and rainbows." She coughed. "All that love and God stuff isn't for kids like us. We're the victims, remember?"

"You can't be a victim forever, Shannon."

"Says the girl who killed our mother."

"With all my heart, I wish I could have said the right things to stop her."

"Face it, Fi, our lives have been one disaster after another."

"It doesn't have to be that way. God promises that He can use all the bad we've gone through for His good. Don't you see? We're loved. We're wanted. We're forgiven. He'll never leave us. We're His masterpieces."

"Whatever." Shannon stood up. "I feel sick. See you later, sis. Ambrose."

Fiona stared at the blank screen in front of her. Her body broke out in a cold sweat and she trembled. Shannon was going to prison. She couldn't save her.

"Prison will do her good. She'll have to get clean in there." Ambrose stood up. "Let's get out of here."

He held out his hand for Fiona and she took it. He put his arm around her shoulders and gave her a brotherly hug.

She said nothing as they exited the building. When they reached the motorcycle, Ambrose passed her the helmet, so she put it on and mounted the bike. Once they were on the road, the conversation with Shannon played over in her head.

It had been disappointing, but what had she expected? She had hoped Shannon's heart would soften. What she expected was pretty much what she'd gotten.

The words Fiona said had poured from her lips, and she'd

believed them wholeheartedly. She wanted Shannon to know the depth of God's love for her. Shannon needed to understand that she wasn't beyond God's loving hand, that she was precious to the Lord, and that He had great plans for her.

Gabe's words came back to her. *"I could stand here all day telling you that you're more than enough for me, but until you believe it for yourself, until you believe you are who God made you to be, my words mean nothing."*

Why was it so hard to believe the Potter had made her His masterpiece? Why could she believe it for her sister, but not believe it for herself?

Fiona's mind kept spinning as she rode. She'd been so preoccupied, she didn't notice they hadn't taken the same route back. When Ambrose pulled into the Moccasin Lake Nature Park, her eyes widened. As kids, they'd visited this place. Did he remember?

He parked the motorcycle and turned off its loud engine. "You took the day off, right? Thought you could use a little nature break after the horror story called Shannon. Besides, Mom Cat said to be kind to you today. You're suffering from heartbreak, so I need details."

Mental and emotional exhaustion tugged at her soul, and being in touch with nature had always refreshed her spirit, but she didn't look forward to baring her soul to anyone, including Ambrose.

He dug in his saddlebag and produced bug spray. "You're going to need this."

She doused herself before they headed toward the cages where injured birds of prey were kept. Although it was sad to see the birds unable to fly, she did enjoy seeing them up close. Birds, like the feathers, reminded her of God's promise of refuge and hope.

"Tell me what happened the night your mom died." Ambrose had matched his pace to hers. "I've heard bits and pieces but not the whole story."

"You know my mom became depressed after my dad went to prison, right?"

He nodded.

"That night had been unusual. She was in such a great mood. Money had been super tight since Dad left, so we had gotten used to not asking for treats. She bought me a chocolate chip ice cream cone with two scoops. She also gave me her locket, because she said I was growing up to be such a sweet and kind young lady. I was thrilled."

"I bet. What were you, ten?"

"I was barely twelve. Shannon was ten."

"Where was she?"

"She was at a friend's, and Mom kept saying how much she wished we were both there.

"When we got in the car to go home, Mom made me sit in the back. Then, we got on the interstate." Fiona's heart beat against her ribs. "At the fork, she headed straight for the yellow barrels and the concrete divider. I have no idea how fast we were going. I screamed and screamed, but she didn't swerve or brake. I don't remember anything else until I was in the hospital."

Ambrose stopped and turned toward her. "So what does Shannon mean when she said you killed her?"

"Shannon blames me for not talking Mom out of it." Fiona swiped at her tears. "And she's right. I should have seen it. Mom was never happy like that, and she was giving away her things. Those are classic signs that someone is suicidal."

Ambrose took hold of her shoulders and forced her to look at him. "You were twelve. You were just a kid. Your mom was supposed to take care of you."

"You sound like my therapist."

Ambrose shrugged. "It doesn't take a degree to identify 'stupid.'"

They reached the bird sanctuary. One screeched and she whirled to see a red-tailed hawk. A few cages down was a barn owl with nerve damage to his shoulder.

"Hey, look at this one." Ambrose pointed to a black vulture. "And in a previous life, I might have said something inappropriate about his poop, but honestly you see this sign that says that vultures' feces acts like a sanitizer and that enzymes in the vulture's digestive tract kill nearly all bacterium and viruses?"

"I'll tuck that away for my upcoming *Jeopardy* appearance." She laughed, grateful to have moved away from the heavy topic of her mother's death. "Speaking of Jeopardy, what would you answer if the category was Birds of Prey and the answer was 'venue'?"

Ambrose arched an eyebrow. "What is a jealous bridesmaid?"

She playfully swatted his arm. "The answer to 'venue' is 'What are a group of vultures called?'"

"You have got to be kidding me. A group of crows is a 'murder' but vultures are a 'venue.' Who makes up this stuff?"

"And a group of owls is a 'parliament.'"

"It figures." He shook his head. "So, Brainiac, what's a group of Harley riders called?"

"Trouble."

They both chuckled and moved on to the next set of cages. They viewed a great horned owl named Lulu, a barred owl, whose vision had been damaged at some point, and of course, a buzzard. Her favorites to watch were the peacocks, who could come and go from their pen, making loud, high-pitched cawing noises. A male stopped in front of her, and proudly displayed his colorful plumage. In the distance, a female returned his cry.

If only relationships were that easy for humans. At least Gabe had his part down. He sure knew how to strut his stuff.

"You were thinking of that Gage guy."

"Gabe, and yeah, I was."

Ambrose nodded his head toward the directional sign. "Let's head down to Moccasin Lake."

They left the cages and followed the path. They crossed over the boardwalk bridge and paused to hear the gurgle of the creek beneath their feet. When she wanted to stop to put her hand on the checkerboard bark of an enormous live oak, Ambrose didn't grumble, but pointed to the ball moss hanging limply from its far-reaching branches. "Remember when you used to be scared of that moss?"

"It was spooky looking."

When she arrived at the lake, they walked across the boards onto the Brigham Dock. A large turtle swam by, and in the distance, Ambrose thought he saw an alligator creep into the water.

Gabe would enjoy this place. Maybe he'd ridden his bike here on the trail at some point.

"So, out with it. Every time we pause, it's like you transport to somewhere on the other side of the world. Tell me what happened with this Gage guy."

"Gabe." She sighed. "And you don't want to hear about my love life."

He leaned against the railing. "Why not? One of us needs to have a love life and mine is currently non-existent."

"I'm sure I could fix you up with a nice nurse."

"Fiona, you're changing the subject."

She sat down on a bench. To her surprise, Ambrose listened carefully as she briefly detailed the last month with Gabe and why she had to break up with him.

"You understand, don't you?" She looked up at Ambrose. "He's too good. His family is too good. Eventually, he'll see I'm not good enough for him."

"So you broke up with him before he could reject you?"

"No...yes...I don't know, maybe." Fiona's breath seemed to catch in her chest.

"Fiona, you're a little bit of a hypocrite."

"What?" She stood and spun toward him.

"Today, you told Shannon that she was a new creation. She was a masterpiece. Do you believe Shannon is God's masterpiece, but you're not?"

She crossed to the other side of the dock and stared out at the water. She wrapped her arms around herself, willing the tears to stay at bay.

Ambrose propped his foot on one of the dock's rail boards. "You're scared, Fiona, and I get it."

There it was. That was the root of her every insecurity. Fear. She was afraid of abandonment. She was afraid of failing. She was afraid of desperation. And more than anything, she was afraid of being rejected—again.

Is that why she pushed Gabe away? To keep him from rejecting her when he saw the real Fiona? She'd made it look like she was doing it for his own good, but was it? Had Ambrose pegged it perfectly?

She rubbed her damp face with her open palms. She'd said her life was a mess, but it was she who'd made this mess. She'd pushed Gabe away.

Ambrose sat down on the bench. "Think about a beautiful pot you've created on your potter's wheel. You love how you shaped it into what you had pictured in your mind. You loved creating something usable, and you love how it turned out, but then the pot turned and said, 'I'm not a special pot. I'm not worthy." He paused. "That's what you're doing. You're a chosen vessel and you're telling God you're not enough."

"I don't feel like a vessel. I feel like more of cracked pot."

"Maybe so, but if you glue a pot back together, what happens when you put a candle inside." He took Fiona's hand and pulled her down beside him. "I haven't been a Christian as long as you, but I've learned one thing: God's love can shine through our brokenness and we foster kids have plenty of that. I think you have to decide if you're going to let God glue your pieces together or if you're going to keep thinking He can fix everyone else, just not you."

Hot tears escaped down her cheeks.

"You are not a victim, Fiona McGrath. You preached it to me for years, but do you truly believe it?"

Fiona nodded slowly, then lifted her damp face toward her brother. "I do."

"Save those words." He nudged her with his shoulder. "After you talk to Gage, you may need them."

"Gabe."

"Yeah, I'd better start getting that right." Ambrose stood. "Okay, that's more talking than I've done in a month. Let's ride."

Fiona walked beside him down the trail, feeling lighter than she had in weeks. Why hadn't she seen this earlier? God had already turned the worst night of her life into the inspiration to work at a job that brought her so much joy. Had anger, bitterness, and resentment silently been building in the deepest corners of her heart until they'd blinded her to God's promises?

A majestic bald eagle soared over the lake, and she recalled the verse in Isaiah, "Those who hope on the Lord shall renew their strength. They will soar on wings like eagles."

It was time for her, once and for all, to turn her hurt into hope.

CHAPTER 28

Fiona stepped out of the car at Mom Cat and Duane's and headed up their walk. Mom Cat had called and asked her to join them for supper.

She knocked, then opened the door. What was she going to tell Mom Cat about the fire building inside her? Every evening, Fiona had poured over the homework her therapist had assigned her. The scriptures seemed to come alive in a fresh new way. It wasn't like a sudden zap of healing, but she could feel the hurt places being slowly mended as never before.

"How's school?" Fiona plopped mashed potatoes onto her plate.

Solana looked at Mom Cat, but Talia took a sudden interest in her napkin. Apparently, the foster care honeymoon was over.

"Talia has to spend some time doing community service. We were hoping maybe she could work in your playroom."

Fiona smiled. "I think we could arrange that. What'd you do, Talia?"

"That school is stupid."

"I've certainly felt that way before." Fiona poured gravy over her mashed potatoes.

"They assigned her a paper on her greatest hurt." Mom Cat put her hand on Talia's. "I think it triggered a lot of feelings."

"I bet." Fiona looked at Talia. "You're going to have to face your greatest hurt, but you shouldn't have to do it in front of an English teacher if you don't want. You should be able to choose who knows your story. I'm not sure I'll still be at Bryce Memorial, but I'll find a place for you to do your hours."

After they'd finished dinner, instead of starting on the dishes, Mom Cat picked up an envelope off the counter. "This came for you, Fiona."

Fiona's eyes narrowed. The handwriting seemed unfamiliar. She took the envelope, which felt thick in her hands. She pulled out a letter and something fell to the floor with a delicate chinking sound.

Her locket! She bent and picked it up, examining the photo of her parents inside to see if was still intact.

"Are you going to read the letter? If you want privacy, we understand."

"No, Mom Cat, I want to share this with you—with all of you." She opened the letter and read the contents aloud.

Dearest Fiona,

I ran into your sister and saw she had this locket. I remembered from the letters you sent me that it was one of your most cherished possessions. When I saw Shannon wearing it, I asked for it back. I didn't know how to get it to you, but I still had your foster parents' address, so I took my chances.

Fiona, I know I've failed you in so many ways. I'm in a half-way house now, but when I get settled and get a job, I want to talk to you if you're willing. You have always been my brightest star. You softened my heart from the first time I held you, and if I hadn't been so selfish, I'd have had the privilege of watching you become the woman you are. I have never stopped loving you, and you may not believe this, but I pray for you and Shannon daily.

Love,
Your father

Fiona's hands shook as she looked down at the paper. Mixed emotions assaulted her from every angle, but her father loved her. He'd prayed for her, and he'd remembered her letters. Just like her heavenly father, he'd not abandoned her.

CHAPTER 29

It had been nearly two weeks since Fiona had last talked to Gabe, but today she had a delivery to make to him. She glanced down at the parcel on her desk and realized she didn't know his address. He'd been to her place, but she'd never been to his.

It was risky, but she'd have to ask Gerri. She'd visit in person. It would be too easy for Gerri to turn her down on the phone.

She opened her door to leave her office and found Gabe's brother standing outside her door. "Mr. Cavenaugh?"

"Chip." He motioned to her office with a nod of his head. "Do you mind if I come in and talk to you?"

"Please do." She stepped back and waved him inside.

He surveyed the room. Several boxes lined one wall. "Going somewhere?"

"The CFO, William Case, informed me that my last day will be at the end of the week."

He seemed to study her clothes. A pair of apple green shorts over polka dotted tights with rainbow striped suspenders. Instead of a hat, she'd pulled her hair into a side ponytail.

"It's Wacky Wednesday." She sighed, but didn't add that this was her last one.

"You might want to hold up on the packing. I don't think you're going to lose your job." Chip cleared his throat. "Gabe found some inconsistencies within the pharmacy department. He's been working with the FBI to get to get the bottom of it. They made the arrests today."

"Who was it? What had they done?"

"I think he'd want to tell you." Chip stuffed his hands in his pockets. "I'm not sure what happened between you two, but he's miserable. He's saved your job. I think you at least owe him a face to face."

"I was already planning to speak with him today, but I don't have his address."

"He's downstairs. Gerri will show you in."

"If I'm lucky," she mumbled.

"She's not part of your fan club?"

"Not anymore."

Chip straightened his shoulders. "Go on. He's miserable, and I think you are, too."

She picked up the package on the desk, her heart pounding at the thought that Gabe was right there in the building. "Can you lock up after me?"

"Sure. Just get out of here."

She paused at the door when she saw her scooter. Should she take it? It would be faster? She placed the box in the basket and took off toward the elevator.

She rolled up to the desk. "Gerri, can you tell me to where Gabe is?"

The administrative assistant didn't look up from her computer monitor. "He's in his office. Third door on the right."

Fiona rolled her eyes. She knew where Gabe's office was, so she didn't need the directions, but why was Gabe here? Her hopes surged. Had Mr. Case changed his mind? Still, when she got to what had been Gabe's office, the room was empty.

She turned and Gerri was standing in the hall, grinning broadly.

"Third door. Not the second."

Fiona made her way down the hall to William Case's office. She knocked on the door and heard a male voice say, "Enter."

She came to an abrupt halt as soon as the door opened. Her eyes widened. William Case wasn't sitting behind the desk, Gabe was.

"Fiona." Gabe stood and came around the desk. "What are you doing here?"

"I could ask you the same." She clutched the back of a chair with her hand.

"I'm the new interim CFO." He motioned her to the chair, then leaned on the corner of his desk. "Remember the Cromoxicillin we talked to Dr. Casanova about in the ER? I worked with the FBI to find out that the hospital had been billed around a hundred seventy-five thousand dollars for it, but it was a fake drug. The hospital pharmacist had set up a dummy corporation, with himself as the president, and billed through that. He's been arrested."

"And Case? Was he involved?"

"Only by ignorance. He insisted he'd gone over everything meticulously, but he missed this. The board voted no-confidence in him and I was temporarily given his position."

Her throat tightened. "Temporarily?"

"It's how they do things."

"I see." She stood and handed him the package.

"What's this?"

"Open it. Trust me."

He tore a strip of packing tape off and reached inside the box.

"Careful," she warned.

He peeled off the bubble wrap and held the vessel out. "My bowl. You painted it." He frowned. "It's been broken."

She took it from him. "I know. I did my best to glue it back together, but it's not perfect." She set it on his desk and withdrew a tealight candle and lighter from the box. She set the candle in the bowl, lit it, and then, shut the lights off in the office.

"Okay, that's cool, Fi. You do realize candles are illegal in the hospital." He traced the ruffled edge of the bowl with his finger. "Why are you showing me the cracked bowl?"

"Do you want to throw it away?" she asked.

"No, I think it's even better this way. Why?"

She drew in a long breath. "Because it's like me. I'm a cracked pot."

"Fiona, I told you until you could believe you're enough yourself, then—"

She placed his hand on his arm. "Please, let me finish. I'm a cracked pot. Life has broken me, and I'll always have scars, but God has put me back together. I know that now, and His light can show through my broken places. I am enough because I'm His."

Even in the candlelight, she saw Gabe smile. He grabbed her suspenders and pulled her close. His hands spanned her waist, making her heart skip.

He kissed her forehead. "My little cracked pot, you are not just enough. You are more than enough in every way."

Then, he lowered his lips to hers and kissed her in a way that left no doubts in her head or in her heart.

Dear Reader Friends,

Thank you for choosing to read *More Than Enough*. I'm honored that you selected this book, and I pray Fiona and Gabe's story of redemption touched your heart.

This story came to be after my niece, Jaclyn, suggested a child life specialist as a character. Her son, Mason, was diagnosed two years ago with osteosarcoma at the age of thirteen. The road has not been an easy one, but the child life specialists worked hard to be a friendly face of normalcy in the crazy world of the hospital.

No book makes it onto the page without being touched by several hands. I have been blessed to have a supportive group around me, and I want to show them the appreciation they deserve by extending a heartfelt thank you...

... to Judy Miller, my dear friend, for her excellent brainstorming and critiquing.

... to my daughter, Caroline, for finding all the little holes and flubs in the storyline.

... to Lesley McDaniel of Lesley Ann McDaniel Editing for her eagle-eyed catches.

... to George at ThinkCap for his great cover work.

...to my niece, Jaclyn, for suggesting a child life specialist as a character.

... to The Mosaic Collection authors for their encouragement on this writing journey.

...to my husband, David, who is always my number one supporter.

... to God, who is above all and in all. All glory belongs to Him.

ABOUT THE AUTHOR

Lorna Seilstad brings history back to life using a generous dash of humor. She is a Carol Award finalist and the author of the **Lake Manawa Summers** series and the **Gregory Sisters** series. Her stories are also part of several novella collections. When she isn't eating chocolate, she teaches women's Bible classes, volunteers with 4-H, and is a wedding planner. She and her husband have three adult children and live in Iowa. Learn more about Lorna at www.lornaseilstad.com.

LET'S CONNECT!

Find Lorna online at www.lornaseilstad.com, and on Facebook and Goodreads.

For news and encouragement about upcoming books, contests, giveaways, and other activities, sign up for Lorna's monthly newsletter.

If you've enjoyed *More Than Enough,* please consider leaving a review on Amazon and Goodreads. Your words bring hope and encouragement to the author as well as to other readers.

Other Books
BY LORNA SEILSTAD

THE GREGORY SISTERS SERIES

When Love Calls
While Love Stirs
As Love Blooms

THE LAKE MANAWA SUMMERS SERIES

Making Waves
A Great Catch
The Ride of Her Life

NOVELLA COLLECTIONS

Seven Brides for Seven Texans
Seven Brides for Seven Texas Rangers
First Love Forever Romance Collection
Victorian Christmas Brides Collection
Cowboys of Summer

Coming Soon

TO THE MOSAIC COLLECTION

One man running from his past, two women he's attracted to, and a peculiar town that won't let him go.

Matthew Sadler rides his '77 Harley into Happenstance, intent on passing through, but people and events conspire to prevent his leaving.

The elderly Barlow sisters consider Matt their knight on a motorcycle. Matt is entranced by Roni, the other lodger at the Happenstance Hotel, who bears an uncanny resemblance to his beloved, deceased wife. The young doctor in town, Paula Percy, adores Matt's motorcycle. However, she is suspicious of Roni, and the feeling is mutual.

As the days pass, the quaint little town, with its unique residents, begins to show its sinister side. When evidence of multiple thefts leads to Matt's door, he must deal with a mystery and yet more false accusations.

Do the old diaries of Amanda Rutherford Barlow hold the answers Matt so desperately seeks? Will Happenstance finally let him go, or does he have a reason to stay?

ABOUT JANICE L. DICK

Janice L. Dick was born and raised in southern Alberta, Canada, into an ethnic Mennonite farm family. She has always loved stories of family heritage and the emigration of her people from Russia. Her aim is not only to share the faith journeys of her forebears, but also to showcase God's sovereignty in the midst of that milieu. Besides historical fiction, Janice writes contemporary novels and short stories, blogs, articles and book reviews. Janice is the winner of the 2016 Janette Oke Award.